SWYNMOOR

Joelle Mellon

Published by Waystone Books
www.waystonebooks.com

ISBN: 0692284036
ISBN-13: 978-0692284032

For Danny
You taught me to have a sense of humor about nearly everything.

CONTENTS

ACKNOWLEDGMENTS

I greatly appreciate the help of several people who encouraged me to continue on with writing this book. I am eternally grateful to Jon, who told me what he thought of my initial drafts, and then put up with my ignoring him while I improved them. I appreciate the patience of my parents and sister, who understood that I had work to do, even though I'd flown across the country to see them. My cats, Meru and Gambit, also tolerated many hours of not being petted while I typed away. I owe a profound debt of gratitude to P.G. Wodehouse (*Jeeves and Wooster*), Terry Pratchett (*Discworld*), and Julian Fellowes (*Downton Abbey*), whose writing styles I shamelessly pilfered. Finally, I'd like to thank Andrew, who asked me to do this work in the first place.

1

Kerris sighed. It was apparently going to be one of those days. She'd lifted the lid from the enormous pickling crock, removed the heavy stone weights that were holding the peppers beneath the brine and peered hopefully at its contents. A thick, fuzzy layer of bluish-white mold was floating nastily on top of the salted water, giving off an odor that smelled unsettlingly like dirty socks. She had been so careful with this batch, too! Pickling crocks were lined up like soldiers against the cellar walls as far as the eye could see, but she was sure that, once again, hers were the only ones that had gone off. There was nothing for it. If she didn't want to spend another month eating stale bread as a punishment, she would simply have to do something about this. And the sort of "something" that she intended meant a trip to the library.

Hurriedly, she replaced the weights and lid before any of the sisters came bustling down the stairs. She dashed up from the cellar, thoughtlessly sure-footed on the treacherous stairs. Her feet knew where every crumbling bit of stone was, as well as every step that was wider or narrower than the others. She had lived at Swynmoor Abbey since she had been a tiny baby, left at the front gate by someone who did not feel up to the task of raising a child in a year when the harvest had been particularly poor. She opened the door to the first floor, then rushed along the corridor, being careful not to actually run, so that the brown-robed nuns would not chastise her. She was going fast enough that a few dark glances and furrowed brows crossed the faces of several of the sisters as she passed, but they didn't actually say anything about it. The abbey was a holy place, and its inhabitants were always supposed to move with a kind of calm dignity. A few of the other Foundlings, who wore simple grey dresses with white aprons like her own, glanced at her curiously, but most ignored her as they went about their business. She rushed up several flights of stairs, breathing rapidly with the exertion by the time she reached the correct floor.

Thankfully, the library was empty, but Kerris knew she had to move quickly if she wanted to be done with her task before Sister Felicity, the librarian, returned from breakfast. Luckily, she knew exactly which book she needed. She grabbed the key from the top drawer of the desk, where Sister Felicity always kept it. Quickly unlocking one of the many cases lining the walls, she pulled the correct small manuscript from the shelf and tucked it into the voluminous pocket of her apron. She was about to lock the books up when she realized that she would probably also need an Old Reachian dictionary if she really wanted to understand what she was reading. She opened it again, grabbed the needed book, then closed and locked the case as rapidly as she could. Managing to replace the key before Sister Felicity arrived, she shoved the dictionary into her other pocket and dashed back down the stairs.

Hoping to avoid as many people as possible, Kerris took the rear corridor to the door that led to the cellar stairs. She made her way down to the pickling crocks. Opening the lid of her crock and removing the stone weights once again, she let out a sigh of relief -- no one had discovered her before she could do what was needed. Taking the manuscript from her apron pocket, she began paging through the last third of it. She knew that the pickle spell was toward the back of the purloined book, but she couldn't remember which page, exactly. She concentrated, translating the Old Reachian words as best she could under the circumstances. She was better than any of the other Foundlings in her class at reading the ancient language, but she had still only studied it for a few years. Suddenly, the Foundling girl came across the word for "pickle" in one of the spells' titles. Ah, that must be it! Just as she began to read the rest of the page, she heard the door at the top of the stairs open. There was no time! Not completely understanding what she was saying, Kerris quickly read the Old Reachian words, simultaneously moving her right hand over the crock in some approximation of a stirring motion. Much to her delight, as soon as the last syllable had been spoken, the mold disappeared, and the only smell wafting from the crock was the salty, tangy scent of pickled peppers. Just as the footsteps reached the lowest of the steps, she remembered to stuff the book back into her apron.

"Kerris Seaborn, what are you doing down here?"

She turned to see Sister Goldrose, who was in charge of pickle making, bearing down on her like an avenging angel.

"J-just checking on my pickles, Sister."

"I heard you were rushing around upstairs like the abbey was on fire."

"I just wanted to be sure that I had time to see how my batch was doing before class started."

The nun sighed. She understood that looking after the Foundlings was an important part of God's work, but the girls drove her halfway to madness sometimes.

"Well, how are they? Spoiled like the last two times you made them? You should really learn to be more care-"

"Actually, this batch seems to be doing well."

Sister Goldrose looked into the crock. Just as the girl said, there was no mold, and the pickled peppers smelled fine. Pulling the sleeve of her brown robe above her elbow, she plunged an arm into the brine and pulled out a pickle. She heard the girl gasp beside her. Although the pepper was firm to the touch, as it should have been, it was also as blue as the sky above.

"Oh no!" wailed Kerris.

"Don't go getting too upset, now. These seem right enough, though the color is rather odd. Tell you what -- we won't sell this batch, but we'll pack it up to send to the castle for our taxes. Won't do those high and mighty folks any harm to eat a few blue pickles."

"Really?"

"You're improving, with God's help, anyhow. Wouldn't have fed your last batch to a dog. Perhaps next time you can make sure they stay red."

Kerris nodded, nearly starting to cry with relief.

"It's just as well that your batch is going to the castle, anyhow. I spoke to Mother Superior about you."

The girl looked horrified for a moment, assuming the worst.

"Not to complain about your pickle-making. No, actually, it was about a bit of a -- reward, since you've been doing so well with your studies. Even your peppers have improved."

"Oh?"

"We thought that you might like to go to the castle this year. You could greet the rich folks in Old Reachian, and make the traditional speech that always accompanies the delivery of our taxes. What do you say?"

Kerris bounced on her heels several times until, unable to contain her excitement, she threw her arms around the nun for a big hug. Sister Goldrose gently pried the girl off of her. Foundlings.

"Very well, then. You can leave tomorrow with Brother Eustace."

The next day, some monks came to the abbey to dump the pickle crocks into barrels, seal them, and load them onto wagons for their destinations. Sister Goldrose strutted proudly among them, rather imperiously telling the monks where each of the barrels was headed. The most perfectly pickled cucumbers, cabbage, peppers, beets, watermelon rind, and eggs were would go North, to be sold at the Harvest Fair. The proceeds would easily keep the abbey funded for the next year, if not more. People eagerly waited for the nuns' pickles each year, and not even so much as a cucumber seed would be left by the fair's end. Those that were only slightly less ideal would be sent to the monastery, for the monks to enjoy throughout the coming winter months. Batches that contained unevenly cut vegetables or had just a pinch too much salt remained at the abbey for the nuns.

The ones that were edible, though not nearly as delicious as the rest, were sent to Swynmoor Castle, for the annual taxes that the nuns rather grudgingly paid to the nobles for allowing them to operate the abbey on their land. They felt no need to give those idle, stuck-up aristocrats anything better than the batches that had made it through the pickling process without spoiling. Any crock that had mold floating on the top or smelled bad would be unceremoniously dumped into the nearby stream, and its creator would be placed on stale bread and water rations for a month. The nuns depended on the pickles as a source on income far too much to tolerate anyone's carelessness in making them.

Kerris stood out in the courtyard, watching the burly monks carrying or even rolling the barrels, as their horses cropped the grass and stamped occasionally. Each year, she enjoyed their bustling efficiency when they came to load up the wagons. It was one of the few times that she ever got to see a man. Cloistered in the abbey with the nuns and the other female Foundlings, she only heard the voices of women and girls nearly all year 'round. She enjoyed listening to the deeper tones of the monks and marveling at how easily they hefted the heavy, sloshing barrels into the wagons. And this year, when they left, she would be going with them. She could scarcely believe that she had been chosen to make the speech at Swynmoor Castle. She often wondered what it was like for women who had been raised outside of the abbey, who lived among their fathers, brothers, and husbands every day. Sister Goldrose strode over to stand beside her, supervising as the last barrels were loaded. Kerris smiled. She thought that the nun secretly enjoyed bossing the men around, even though she often complained about them after they left.

"Careful with that barrel, Brother!" she shouted at one of them.

He merely shook his head bemusedly and carried on with his work. Raising her arms briefly in a "what-can-I-do-with-them" gesture, Sister Goldrose turned to the Foundling girl and gently pinched her cheek.

"You be careful, out there in the world," she admonished, "There's plenty of wicked men outside the gates of the abbey, and no shortage of wicked women, either."

"I will."

"I know you'll do us all proud with your speech. Be sure to remember as much as you can about the castle and the people you meet there. The other girls will want to hear all about them when you return."

"Yes, Sister Goldrose,"

4

"That's our girl."

The nun reached into the pocket of her robe, pulling out a large, shiny apple and a hunk of cheese.

"You probably won't arrive until nearly sunset, so here's a bit of food for the journey. Enjoy your time away from us -- but not too much."

Kerris nodded.

"Off you go, then."

Just after a large, smiling monk swung himself up into the wagon and took the horses' reins, Kerris clambered up to join him.

"Watch out for the girl, Brother Eustace," the nun said at last, "'Twill be her first time at the castle."

"Never fear, Sister," he replied.

As he gently snapped the reins, Kerris reached into her apron pocket to put the food away for later. Much to her surprise, she encountered something solid and hard beneath her fingertips. The books! In her excitement about going to Swynmoor Castle, she'd forgotten to sneak them back into the library. As she watched Sister Goldrose becoming increasingly smaller in the distance, she said a silent prayer that Sister Felicity wouldn't notice they were gone before she was able to return them.

Tom sighed. It was apparently going to be one of those days. On the first afternoon of the harvest season, two extremely urgent messages were delivered to Swynmoor Castle. The sweating, panting couriers had practically collapsed at the front gates, exhausted from nonstop riding across the plains. The first messenger had arrived from the South, and the letter he bore said that Reynaud the Black was rapidly approaching, intent on attacking the castle with his terrible army of ogres and Fomorians. The second rider had come from the West, bringing the message that Tom's Aunt Jilona would also soon be descending upon the castle. She was planning to stay for several weeks and would be accompanied by a girl named Topaz Stonemont. Tom's formidable aunt believed that the young lady would make an excellent bride for him. He held a letter in each hand, staring at them with a rapidly rising sense of dread, trying to decide which was worse. Under the circumstances, the best he could hope for was that Reynaud would show up first, forcing his aunt to turn back. At least then, Tom thought, there would be only one threat to his well-being and sanity to contend with.

"Honestly," his mother, Glynis, fussed, when he gave her the bad news, "Your aunt has always had the worst timing. What are we to do? Nearly all the servants are away in Brookmeade for the Harvest Ball. If I serve her nothing but the cold sandwiches they left for us, she'll disinherit you."

"I don't know that it will matter much if Reynaud the Black's army destroys the castle, mother. It seems much worse for us that nearly all the guards are at the ball, as well," Tom replied.

Thoughtfully, he tapped the nib of a quill pen against his chin, making a blotch of ink appear on his face. He was trying to work out whether he could possibly get a message to his aunt about Reynaud in time, so that she would be deterred. It was probably hopeless. From what the messenger had said, she and that dratted girl would only be a couple of hours away by now. At least there would be time for a messenger to get to Brookmeade, so that the castle staff would know that they had to stay on. With a hostile army rapidly approaching, it would surely be too dangerous for them to return.

"Honestly, that's another thing!" his mother interrupted his thoughts, "How does she expect us to defend Swynmoor to begin with when she only sends such a paltry amount of money? It would serve her right if Reynaud did manage to pull the place down around our ears."

Tom frowned and looked out the window anxiously, but no one seemed to be approaching from either the South or the West. From the East, however, a small caravan of wagons loaded with seemingly countless barrels was lumbering across the grassy plain, making its way directly toward the castle.

"Now what?" he muttered.

After a few moments, Waltham, one of the few servants who were too old to be interested in attending balls, harvest-related or otherwise, made his way into the room and bowed, his joints creaking audibly.

"There are monks at the front gate, m'lord. They've come to deliver the annual tax pickles from the abbey."

"Oooh, that's nice," Glynis enthused, "I've been positively longing for some salty pickled cabbage, and we ran out of last year's tax pickles months ago."

Tom made a face.

"I don't know how you can eat that stuff. Honestly, mother, if father hadn't passed on years ago, I'd worry that you were pregnant."

"Tell the monks that they can put the barrels in the cellar, as they do every year. And do encourage them to stay for a bit after they've unloaded -- at least until supper. It's only cold sandwiches, but I don't think they'll mind. The servants always leave us far too much food when they go to a dance or a faire or something."

"Are you really sure that's wise? Reynaud the Black is apparently threatening to descend upon us like --"

Tom paused for a moment, searching for an appropriate comparison.

"Like a bout of indigestion from pickled cabbage. Not to mention Aunt Jilona showing up, no doubt with her entire pack of rat-sized dogs, as well as some completely unmarriageable spinster girl. Honestly, the day is absolutely ruined, if not the whole week."

"Don't sulk, Tom -- it's unbecoming. We mustn't be rude to men of God, no matter who else may be arriving."

"Very well then," he said, a bit resentfully, "Tell them that they're invited to stay for supper."

"Yes, m'lord," said Waltham.

The servant bowed again, in spite of his protesting joints, before leaving the room.

"Perhaps they can pray that God spares us from Aunt Jilona -- not to mention Toenail -- or whatever her name is. Or Reynaud the Black. At this point, I almost don't care who we're spared from, as long as we're spared from somebody."

Reynaud sighed. It was apparently going to be one of those days. Somehow, he just couldn't imagine this happening to his father or his older brothers. But he was the just the third son, of course, which meant that no one ever felt they had to listen to him, even if he was supposed to be in command. Not that he'd wanted to be in charge, anyway. As usual, it was all his father's idea. Izir, the Fomorian general, all eight feet of him, had lumbered over to Garrok, the ogre general. He'd bent down so that his face was inches away from the ogre's, and Izir was staring him down with his one good eye. No doubt, Reynaud thought, both of them had unbelievably awful breath. He didn't know how they managed not to pass out from being that close to each other.

"What did you say?" demanded the Fomorian, glaring at Garrok.

The ogre bristled like the boar he somewhat resembled, thrusting his lower tusks out toward Izir's remaining good eye.

"I said -- that the rabbits we caught will be divided equally."

The Fomorian shook his head, heedless of the proximity of his rival's tusks. He jammed a warty grey finger into Garrok's broad, furry chest.

"We did not catch anything. Ogres did not hunt. Ogres stayed behind, to build fires and cook our prey -- like woman. You cook like woman, you eat like woman -- when hunters have finished!"

"Izir. Garrok. Surely there's a way --" Reynaud tried to interrupt.

"Be quiet, human. This does not concern you," the ogre said, menacingly.

"Um, well. I hate to interrupt, but it actually does. You've both sworn fealty to me, as your commander, so --"

Izir turned his attention from Garrok to bring himself up to his full, terrifying height again and stalk over to where Reynaud was standing. That was progress, at least, though not exactly the sort he had in mind. He suddenly realized that, as the Fomorian general was walking, he was also reaching over his head for the handle of the enormous battle axe that he always kept firmly strapped to his back.

"Izir -- that's not a very good idea. Remember that your king told you --"

Without another word, the enormous creature raised the weapon above his head. Before Reynaud could even decide which way to dodge, the Fomorian had brought the blade down firmly. It connected with an enormous, gnarled branch, which was about ten feet up the thick trunk of a tree that was directly behind Reynaud. Fortunately, although his brain took a few moments to comprehend what was happening, his instincts took over. He dove out of the way before the branch could hit him, though it meant landing hard on his chest with his arms and legs flailing.

"Now see here!" he shouted.

He tried to sound at least somewhat threatening, despite being splayed out awkwardly on the ground, but it just didn't work. Izir picked him up in his enormous, grey, wart-covered hands and hung the back of his shirt from the remainder of the branch, which was now chopped into something resembling a spike. The shirt, which was quite expensive, ripped in the spot where the wood penetrated it, but the fabric was still strong enough to hold him aloft. Renaud kicked his feet ineffectually, suspended in the air. He felt like a pair of pants that had been hung on a washing line to dry. Grinning horribly, the Fomorian turned and stomped back over to the ogre. He threw his axe onto the ground and put his fists up like a boxer.

"Settle this, if not too woman to fight," he grunted.

The ogre grinned and tossed his sword into the grass, then tucked his head down and lunged at the Fomorian. Garrok's metal helmet connected viciously with Izir's chest, and the two fell to the ground, rolling around, fists flying. Almost immediately, of course, several of the foot soldiers noticed what was happening. They stood up from their cooking fires and came running over, pounding the grass and earth under their gigantic feet.

"Fight! Fight!" the cry went up, attracting even more ogres and Fomorians.

"Bloody Hell," the young man cursed.

He squirmed around, trying to get hold of his sword, which his father, embarrassingly enough, had named Darkheart when he'd ceremonially bestowed it upon Reynaud. It sounded like the weapon of a stock villain from a ballad. As he struggled, he fumed to himself once again that he had warned his father it was a bad idea to hire mercenaries, especially non-human ones, but of course, the old man wouldn't listen. This was the result. Ah. There was the handle of his sword at last, which would be useful, however absurdly named. He carefully maneuvered so that the blade was behind his neck and began sawing away at the collar of his shirt. He cursed again under his breath as he heard the fabric tearing -- he'd liked that shirt. He braced himself for the fall as the cloth gave way entirely, taking care to move his sword well away from his throat just before the moment of truth came, and he dropped to the ground.

He landed with impressive agility, somehow managing to neither turn his ankle nor accidentally stab himself with the naked sword. It was the first thing that had gone right for him all day. He looked over at the cluster of soldiers, some pumping their fists in the air, others banging their blades against their shields and all cheering on their respective brawling generals. It was like being in one of the worst taverns imaginable. He tried to move quietly, although he doubted if the mercenaries would have noticed him if he'd started singing at the top of his lungs. He crept over to the traps, where the rabbits were huddled together, chewing grass nervously. One by one, he opened the doors of each of the wooden cages. The animals stared at him, too terrified to move.

"Well, go on," he hissed.

Finally, he had to pick a couple of them up and set them in the grass, practically pushing them from behind into freedom. At last, they got the idea and began hopping away. He let them get more than halfway to the woods.

Then, he shouted, "Hey, your dinner -- it's getting away!"

As he suspected, no one took any notice of him. Muttering, he made his way over to the knot of Fomorians and ogres and poked one lightly in the back with his sword. As the creature turned around, he saw that it was an ogre, who looked furious at having his entertainment interrupted.

"Your dinner -- it's getting away!" he repeated.

"Hrrruh?" the mercenary said, anger turning to confusion in its eyes.

"The rabbits -- you know -- for supper -- they're escaping!" he explained.

Finally, comprehension dawned.

"Hey!" he shouted, "The rabbits -- our prey -- they've gotten out!"

Reynaud took up the cry again, "The rabbits are escaping!"

Gradually, the foot soldiers stopped shouting about the fight and began shouting instead about their rapidly fleeing dinner. A few began to break off from the group to run in the direction of the cages.

"Rabbits!" some of them were yelling.

"So hungry!" others shouted.

At last, they all took off to pursue their supper, which was largely outdistancing them, thanks to the head start Reynaud had generously allowed. Even the two generals eventually disengaged from each other long enough to ascertain what was happening and declare a truce long enough to run after the rabbits. Reynaud merely stood aside, rubbing the back of his neck, where the tree branch had scratched it uncomfortably. He watched his father's mercenaries stumble about, the sun setting spectacularly behind them. He took his wineskin from his belt, pulled out the stopper and had a long drink, letting it drip down his chin a bit. They hadn't even reached Swynmoor castle yet, but he could already tell that it was going to feel like a very long siege.

Tom sat at the head of the table, looking with approval at the many platters piled high with sandwiches. They were interspersed with wooden pitchers of ale and small dishes of different types of pickles, most of which, despite his feelings about pickled cabbage, he genuinely liked. The day seemed to be turning out all right after all. Despite the fuss, there had been no sign of either his aunt or Reynaud the Black's army. Better still, they were having sandwiches for dinner, something he had been looking forward to for the better part of a week. This was his idea of a good meal. No fooling about with various courses or cutlery. No delaying your dinner until a servant made his way around the table until he got to your place and served your food. Just sandwiches, pickles, and good, strong ale. Bliss. He was also pleased that he only had to wait a few minutes before his mother came into the great hall and sat near him. He glanced down the length of the rather absurdly huge table, noting with some satisfaction that no other places had been set. No waiting around for anybody else to arrive before eating could begin. He reached a hand toward the nearest platter, wondering if there were any bacon sandwiches. That would make his happiness complete. Before his fingers even touched bread, however, his mother interrupted.

"Tom, dear, before we begin --"

He sighed, "Do you really think we need to say grace just now? There are only two of us tonight, after all."

"No, it's not that, though we probably should, especially with all the monks in the house at the moment. Waltham told me that the girl from the abbey who made some of the pickles is supposed to say a few words to us in Old Reachian. You know, the usual speech that's made when the nuns pay their taxes."

"Does she have to do that now? I'm starving," he protested.

"Well, we should acknowledge their payment before we eat any of their pickles."

"Oh, very well. Send her in."

Glynis picked up a small bell that had been placed next to her eating dagger and rang it. Tom stared at the sandwiches a bit morosely, trying to see if he could detect a bit of bacon sticking out of the side of any of them. He supposed it wouldn't really matter all that much which one he grabbed, unless some were cucumber and butter. With all of the delicious possibilities for fillings, he'd never understood why anyone would ruin a perfectly good sandwich with an un-pickled cucumber. Suddenly, however, he was jarred out of his musings by the arrival of a girl who might possibly have been the loveliest young woman he'd ever laid eyes on.

She was attired in the simple grey dress and apron of a Foundling from Swynmoor Abbey, but he was sure that she could have worn a potato sack and still been positively breathtaking. The garment was intended to be rather generic and shapeless, since it was meant as a sort of uniform to be worn by a girl who would probably, at some point in her future, become a nun. However, this particular Foundling girl managed to fill it out enticingly with her curves, and the modesty of the garment only served to make him even more curious about what it concealed. She had long, honey colored hair which had been pulled into one sleek braid that hung neatly down the back of her slender, white neck. She turned her lovely, amber-colored eyes toward Tom and looked directly at him for a moment, just before she bowed.

"I bring you greetings from Swynmoor Abbey, my lord and lady."

He opened his mouth a little, but he couldn't bring himself to say anything at all in reply. The silence lengthened until it began to hang in the air awkwardly.

"Hello, my dear," said his mother, at last, "As always, we appreciate the pickles. What is your name?"

"Kerris Seaborn, my lady. I've been selected this year to make the traditional speech to you in Old Reachian. Shall I do so now?"

Glynis looked over at her son. As heir to Swynmoor Castle, he was really supposed to be the one who formally gave permission for the speech to be made, but he continued to just sit with a sort of glazed look on his face. If the girl hadn't been standing there, she would have rolled her eyes. She knew he was disappointed about having to delay his supper, but she hadn't expected him to positively sulk like this, no matter how much he loved bacon sandwiches.

"We honor the work of Swynmoor Abbey," the older woman said at last, taking over Tom's traditional line.

Kerris brought her hands together in front of her heart, making a steeple with her fingertips, and briefly cleared her throat.

"Kreloch rygol se --" she began.

She didn't make it much farther before the traditional speech was drowned out by the yapping of what sounded like every Rathound in Highreach.

Just then, Waltham rounded the corner into the great hall, wheezing with exertion.

"Lady Swynmoor and Lady Topaz Stonemont!" he announced.

He had scarcely managed to get the words out of his mouth before at least a dozen poufy little overbred dogs in various shades of white, reddish-brown and black scurried into the room on their tiny, well-manicured paws, many of them barking excitedly in an annoyingly high register. A woman swept imperiously into the great hall behind them. Her grey-streaked black hair was piled almost absurdly high on top of her head, the ridiculous hairstyle accentuating an already prominent narrow, beak-like nose. Her blindingly bright green dress dripped with lace and bows at her elbows and waist, and they also decorated the immodestly low neckline, drawing attention to her ample powdered décolletage. Rings with precious stones the size of eggs glittered on nearly every finger, and her face was caked in makeup that was, if anything, even more shockingly colored than the gown. An enormous green feather had been stuck into the tallest part of her hair, so that it fluttered above the entire ensemble like a garish flag. She was followed by at least a dozen more tiny dogs, as well as a teenage girl who was so tall that she towered over the older woman, despite the enormous hair. Although less absurdly dressed than her companion, she still wore a gown that was a practically phosphorescent shade of pink, and her elaborately braided dark brown hair was festooned with what seemed like an entire bouquet of stemless orange flowers. She, at least, had the good grace to stare at the floor, looking rather embarrassed about the spectacle. They looked like a pair of tropical birds that had flown down from the sky, only to find that they had somehow landed in a climate that was entirely unsuitable for them.

"Glynis!" the older lady practically shouted over the noise of the Rathounds, "You're looking well. A bit rounder in the face, perhaps -- but well, nonetheless!"

"Thank you, Jilona. We didn't hear you arrive."

"How could you, all the way in here. This room is like a crypt, the way outside sound gets muffled by these stones. I always told Malvern that it needed some windows, but he never listened."

"How is he these days?" Tom's mother asked.

"Tiresome. He has gout. And rheumatism. I can't tell you I was entirely sorry to leave him behind in Finbarr Springs."

"I'm sorry to hear that he's still unwell."

"Yes, yes. Get better or die, I always tell him, but he will malinger."

Suddenly noticing the platters, she reached across the table and grabbed a sandwich.

"Thank heavens. I can't tell you how hungry it makes me, riding in that uncomfortable carriage for hours on end. The poor dogs were positively sick for most of the way, weren't you, my babies?"

Scooping up a little white Rathound in one arm, she extracted a piece of bacon from the sandwich and fed it to the animal, who ate it from her fingers delicately. She then took a large bite out of the remaining sandwich. Tom didn't know which was worse -- that Aunt Jilona had interrupted the exquisite young Foundling's speech or that she had helped herself to food when he had been forbidden to eat, a few minutes before. It was just his luck that she managed to get a bacon one, as well. He bit his lip -- hard -- so that he wouldn't say anything that would get him into too much trouble. But he couldn't entirely suppress a groan as Aunt Jilona grabbed an entire platter and put it on the floor for the dogs, who began enthusiastically eating his dinner. He had to admit, though, that at least it made them stop barking. For the first time since she'd arrived, his aunt seemed to notice him.

"Tomlin, there you are, you layabout! You'll be pleased to know that I've brought a young lady for you. Can't let the Moondown line die out entirely, you know."

As if on cue, both Tom and the brightly dressed young girl simultaneously turned red with embarrassment.

"This is Lady Topaz, the daughter of my only real friend at Finbarr Springs. I'd have died of boredom in the first week if I hadn't met this young lady's mother. Topaz, this is my nephew, Tomlin. Perhaps you'll be able to make something of him after you're married."

Thankfully, Tom's mother came to the rescue at last.

"It's a bit soon for that, Jilona. After all, the two of them haven't even said a word to each other."

"No time like the present, I say. Besides, it's best that they marry before they get to know each other too well. Heaven knows, if I'd really understood what I was getting into with Malvern, I would have climbed out the chapel window on our wedding day. Well, say hello to the girl, Tomlin."

"Welcome to Swynmoor Castle, Lady Topaz," he mumbled into his still tragically empty plate.

"Thank you. I'm sure I'll enjoy it here," she replied, looking at the flagstones on the floor.

"That's better," said Tom's aunt, "It's good to be home."

With that, she took another platter and tossed it onto the floor, to the delight of her Rathounds.

Of course, the only sandwiches left for the human beings had been cucumber and butter. Tom's mother and aunt devoured them, while he and Topaz, who apparently shared his dislike of that sandwich filling, had to make do with pickles and ale. Given his limited supper, it was also inevitable that Tom got roaring drunk and eventually had to be helped from the room by Waltham, a man who was so old and creaky that he sometimes needed a cane to walk himself. They both tripped over several dogs on their way out, while Tom's aunt clicked her tongue at him disapprovingly.

After waiting for nearly an hour to give her speech or be dismissed from the room, Kerris eventually bowed to the nobles, who didn't notice, and quietly fled back down to the warmth and relative sanity of the kitchen. It didn't help matters that the monks laughed when they asked her how the speech had gone over, and she had to tell them what happened. The aristocrats hadn't even waited to have their first pickles until after she had finished the speech, as they were supposed to do. Stupid rich people, she thought. Sister Goldrose was right about them.

2

Despite the lack of servants, as well as the hostile army that was rapidly approaching from the South, Tom's aunt had insisted on having one of her excruciating formal teas in the parlor. He was obliged to attend even though he had a pounding headache, an unpleasant souvenir from the previous night's meal of beer and pickles. Exacerbating his misery, the outfits that his aunt and her protégé were wearing were even more eye-searing than they'd been the day before. Even under the best of circumstances, looking at them would have been rather headache-inducing. Aunt Jilona had exchanged her nearly unbearable bright green dress for one that was an equally blinding shade of yellow, with still more lace dripping from the bodice and sleeves. She'd dispensed with the ridiculous green feather that had been in her hair, which should have helped to tone the outfit down. Unfortunately, however, she'd replaced it with an entire stuffed yellow bird, which sat atop the mountain of her hairdo with a startled expression, looking as if it was perpetually in the process of laying an egg. Topaz's dress had been made in a similarly agonizing shade of blue and was trimmed with flashing silver ribbons. Her hair had been liberally sprinkled with paste jewels that had been cut to resemble tiny winking stars. Looking at either of them for too long made Tom feel positively nauseous.

"Aren't the two of you lovely!" his mother exclaimed.

"Why thank you," Aunt Jilona gushed, "Lace and bright colors are the fashion of the moment, you know. I'll have to send you some things when I return to Finbarr Springs. You positively look like a sparrow next to us."

"Wouldn't that be delightful?" Glynis replied.

Trying to block out the thought of his mother wearing a dress that was as appalling as his aunt's, Tom stood and began to make his way over to the low table of refreshments that had been set out for tea. Inevitably, he stumbled as his foot thumped into the side of one of the little dogs. It looked accusingly at him and yapped as discordantly as possible, then scurried away to menace someone else. Tom only managed to suppress a groan because he noticed that a tumbler of whiskey and a glass had been set out for him on the tea table. One of the true privileges of being a man, he thought, was that you could have whiskey at teatime, and no one was supposed to look askance at you. Of course, that didn't stop his mother from doing so, even though she knew very well that it was a privilege he seldom chose to exercise. He positively glared at her in response, which made her turn her attention back to the other ladies. Defiantly, he poured himself a glass, mixing it with only a small amount of water.

He briefly considered having a tea sandwich or two, but he was dismayed to find that they were all cucumber and butter. They were probably leftovers from the night before, though the servants had re-cut them into the little triangles that were most appropriate for teatime. Tom was starving. He'd slept through breakfast and had spent his lunchtime in conference with Waltham, trying to determine what, if any, defenses could be mustered against Reynaud the Black. Ignoring all teatime protocol about tiny food being the ideal, he cut himself a positively enormous slice of almond cake to go with his drink.

"Tomlin," his aunt said, disapprovingly, "You are going to get fat. And then Lady Topaz won't want to marry you after all, will you, dear?"

"And you'll be drunk before the sun sets," his mother chimed in, "Really, it's not like you to drink whiskey at teatime."

"Malvern often took whiskey at teatime," Aunt Jilona added, ominously, clucking her tongue, "And look where it got him. Forced to leave his home to take the waters for his health. Why, he's practically at death's door."

Tom made his way back to his chair and sat down again, managing to avoid the dogs. He took large bite of cake but said nothing in response. As he grew older, he increasingly understood why his Uncle Malvern had been practically silent almost all the time. With Aunt Jilona, anything he said would be used against him. And if eating cake would cause Topaz to like him less, he would make a point of consuming absolute loads of it, he thought petulantly. With her height and that ridiculous dress, she looked like a particularly gaudy Maypole. Tom noted that the food and drink were beginning to dispel the worst of his hangover, but he wisely kept that information to himself, to avoid provoking the women into a full-blown argument.

Before his head entirely stopped throbbing, however, Aunt Jilona had Topaz's little harp brought down from her room, so that she could show off her skill with it. The tuning alone made him clench his teeth. Once she began playing in earnest, he had to admit, she was competent enough. However, if the angels themselves had been strumming away on their harps, they only would have exacerbated the pounding in his head. He drained his whiskey and water, somewhat resigned to never being free of throbbing temples again. At last, when the harp playing was done, he thought that he would be released from the Eternal Teatime. But no, the older ladies insisted that he and Topaz should get to know one another. Meanwhile, his mother and aunt sat at a table only a few yards away, obviously pretending to be too immersed in a complicated card game to hear what the young folks were saying. Not that he was inclined to say anything particularly scandalous to a girl that he'd just met the day before. They stared awkwardly at each other for a moment, then she began twisting her handkerchief while he fiddled with making himself another drink.

"So," he said, examining a piece of ice before dropping it into his glass, "Does your family live in Finbarr Springs?"

"No," she replied, looking positively relieved, "My mother just went to take the waters, like most of the people there. Our estate is a bit further east, near --"

The impromptu geography lesson was interrupted by Waltham, who uncharacteristically flung the door open, allowing it to bang loudly against the wall.

"Whatever can be the meaning of this?" cried Aunt Jilona, indignantly.

"I'm sorry to inform you of this, m'lord and ladies, but Lord Reynaud is at the gates with his army."

"Good heavens! What are we to do?" said Glynis.

"At the moment, the demand is that Lord Tomlin must come out to meet him alone, so that Lord Reynaud can present him with his terms."

Tom stood up a bit unsteadily from the whiskey. Unexpectedly, he found that it came as something of a relief to hear this. It freed him from waiting for the inevitable, as well as providing him with a fantastic excuse to escape from further post-prandial conversation. He drew himself up to his full height (which he suspected was still several inches less than Topaz's) and struck as grand of a pose as he could muster.

"Well, that settles it, then," he said, slurring only a little, "Get out my formal battle clothes and saddle my horse."

"Tom, dear," his mother interjected, "Your formal battle clothes don't fit you anymore. You haven't worn them since you returned home from school a few years ago."

"And you'd best take one of my horses out there. All of yours are so old, I wouldn't be surprised if they collapsed under you in front of Lord Reynaud," his aunt added.

He slumped again, since it was apparently futile to even try to assume any sort of grandiosity. He was going to seem absolutely ridiculous to Reynaud the Black. He sneaked a look from the corner of his eye to see if Topaz was trying to suppress a giggle at his expense. To her credit, she hadn't cracked a smile.

"Very well, then. Saddle one of Lady Swynmoor's horses, and find me -- an outfit that doesn't look too shabby. Oh, and you'd better dust off the house banner. It is the expected thing to carry it in these sorts of situations, after all."

"Very good sir," said Waltham, as he bowed and left the room.

Ultimately, the clothes that the old servant found for him weren't half bad, though they smelled powerfully of mothballs. The outfit had originally belonged to his father; it was the formal one he had worn at his wedding. The pants, shirt, and jacket were entirely white, though the boots and gloves were grey, and only a size or so too big for him. No one would notice, especially if he could manage to stay on his aunt's horse the entire time, so that he wouldn't have to walk in the slightly-too-large footwear. Several medals and family emblems had been pinned to the lapel of the jacket, making it simultaneously more formal and military. The horse Waltham chose for him was also white, which the old man thought would look symbolic. It would contrast sharply with Reynaud's black clothing, as if Tom was silently stating, "I am all that is good and pure, and you are not". His mother came up to kiss him on the forehead and wish him luck before he went out to meet the enemy.

"Don't worry too much, mother," he said gallantly, "This is just the initial meeting of the two sides. If Reynaud did anything against me today, it would be considered quite dishonorable."

"But, Tom dear -- are you sure he's an honorable man?" she asked.

Tom sighed. He hadn't thought of that before. Everything he'd learned at school about military tactics depended on both sides behaving as gentlemen.

"Well," he replied, "There's only one way to find out."

He made his way down to the courtyard and managed to mount his horse with only a small amount of unsteadiness left over from the whiskey. He waved at the very few manservants left at the castle, all of whom had assembled to show him off. Even one of the monks came out and made a traditional gesture of blessing, joining his thumbs and fingers together to form a triangle. Tom looked around to see if he could catch a glimpse of that girl from the abbey who had looked so beautiful the night before, but he had no luck. If he was going to die today, it would be with the last woman he laid eyes on being his mother. After what he hoped was a gallant wave, he took hold of a long pole with a flag bearing the family crest flying from the top. It depicted a crescent moon set against a field of deep blue. It looked noble enough, though it, too, smelled of mothballs. Many years had passed since the last time Swynmoor Castle had defended itself against an onslaught. Still waving, he gently touched his spurs to his horse's flanks and set off as the heavy castle gates were opened and the drawbridge was lowered. His white horse walked at what he hoped was a stately pace down the hill.

Squinting into the setting sun, which seemed determined to blind him, Tom caught his first sight of Reynaud the Black, who was sitting on his mount at the bottom of the hill. Unsurprisingly, yet depressingly, he cut a very fine figure astride the horse, which was, also unsurprisingly, black. He wore black leather armor which was studded with bits of gold, and even his boots and gloves were the color of a midnight sky. Other than the occasional flash of gold on his buckles or bridle, the only thing that broke from his unrelentingly dark color scheme was his family banner, which flew from the top of a long pole that he carried, like his adversary. Ridiculously, the heraldic crest of the noble house of Fynchester seemed to be a brown hedgehog parading boldly across a field of green. Tom blinked a couple of times to make sure that the setting sun in his eyes wasn't deceiving him. But no, the symbol of Reynaud the Black's house really did seem to be a hedgehog.

"Lord Swynmoor, I presume?" the black knight stated calmly.

"Erm, well -- sort of. That's actually my uncle, but he's not here at the moment. He's rather ill, you see --"

The knight gazed at him silently.

"Ahem. You are Lord Reynaud, known as 'the Black', I suppose. Your reputation precedes you."

The other man nodded, then reached into a small saddlebag with his black-gloved fingers. Apparently, however, what he wanted did not immediately come to hand, and he was forced to rummage around a bit. And rummage some more. The horses stamped impatiently.

To break the silence, Tom said, "Excuse me, but is that really a hedgehog?"

"What?"

"On your family crest. Is it a hedgehog? I've been trying to decide if it's just an unfortunately rendered boar or something. But it seems to be --"

"A hedgehog. Yes."

"How ghastly for you! I wonder what went through the first Earl of Fynchester's mind. Ah, that will strike fear into the hearts of our enemies."

"Now see here, Swynmoor --"

"I mean, really -- a hedgehog! An animal that curls up into a ball when threatened and hopes that whatever is after it goes away! That must be extraordinary when the noble houses gather on the field of war. The mighty eagle of the Alwyns, the fierce bear of the Cernan family, and the proud hedgehog of the house of Fynchester. I mean, it rather makes you wonder what your ancestors were drinking, rather than thinking, when you come down to it."

Reynaud burst out at last, "Yours isn't all that terrifying, either! The moon? Threatening to lob green cheese at your enemies, are you?"

"Well," sniffed Tom, rather offended, "At least it's not a hedgehog."

"Ah -- at last!" said Reynaud.

He triumphantly pulled a scroll stamped with a wax seal from his saddlebag and held it aloft.

"My father's terms," the black knight explained, "Have you come to hear them or not?"

"I don't know what else you'd suppose I'm doing out here. Other than escaping from my aunt's tea party."

The other man groaned sympathetically, "Ugh, those are dreadful. When my aunt arrived --"

As if taking offense at the delay, Reynaud's horse, Altairos, snorted particularly loudly. The young man shook himself, reminding himself to seem more imposing.

"Right. Terms."

With a creditable dramatic flourish, he broke the seal and unrolled the scroll.

"The Earl of Fynchester herewith demands that you surrender your lands, castle, and worldly goods unto him. In return, all members of the House of Swynmoor shall be allowed to retire quietly to religious life. Alternately, should they so choose, your family members could depart on a ship for any country of their choosing, provided that it lies across the sea, and provided that all solemnly swear never to return. In exchange for your peaceful surrender, no punishment shall be undertaken. Your family shall not be harmed in any way, and my dread army of ogres and Fomorians shall do no damage to the lands and castle that your family has called its own. If you so agree, you may now swear an oath of fealty to this emissary -- my son Reynaud, who now stands before you."

"You're sitting before me. You know, on a horse."

Rather than dignifying that response with an answer, he rolled the paper up and stuffed it back into the recesses of his saddlebag.

"Well?" the dark knight asked.

"Well, what?"

"Do you surrender to me?"

"My dear chap. My family has lived in this castle for centuries. Surely you don't expect me to just throw it in your lap for a few vague threats, do you?"

"I suppose not."

"Of course I wouldn't."

"I could make some more specific threats," he added, hopefully.

"No, I'm afraid that wouldn't work either."

"I suppose it will have to be a siege, then."

"Yes. It's going to be a long one. This castle was built to withstand them."

Both young men sighed, then looked imploringly at each other for a moment.

At last, Tom tried, "You could always, you know --"

"What?"

"Well -- throw the whole thing over and just bugger off home. I wouldn't tell anyone."

"No, I'm afraid that my father would never stand for that sort of thing. He'd send me straight back here with an even bigger army."

"Very well. I'd best be off then. To tell my family what's in store for them."

He turned his horse back toward the castle.

"Swynmoor --" Reynaud called after him.

Tom stopped and looked back over his shoulder.

"Yes?"

"I really am sorry about this. You seem like a decent chap."

Tom shrugged, "Family obligations. Not much to be done about it."

With that, he turned again toward Swynmoor Castle and rode back up the hill, over the drawbridge, and through the gates. Once inside, he dismounted, and before his feet even touched the ground, he saw that all three of the ladies were rushing toward him, accompanied by an entire kennel's worth of tiny yapping dogs.

"We saw the whole thing from the window!" his mother exclaimed, "You were perfect! You looked like a prince from a ballad!"

"We couldn't hear a thing, of course," his aunt added, "So, what are the demands of the Noble House of Hedgehog?"

"They want us to just turn everything over to them. Lands, castle -- the whole lot. According to Reynaud out there, our family has the brilliant choice of either becoming monks and nuns or being exiled to someplace across the ocean, never to be seen again."

"How dreadful!" said his mother, "What did you tell him?"

"Oh, to stick it up his bottom, more or less."

"Tomlin -- language! There are ladies present!"

"We're at war, Aunt Jilona. Certain pleasantries must be dispensed with now."

She sniffed, "Well, if we don't maintain our civilities, we've already lost."

"That may be inevitable in any case. Unless the king comes to save us, or Reynaud just gives up and goes home, I'm not sure how we can win this one. We hardly kept any soldiers here to begin with, and those few that we had went to the Harvest Ball. Not that I'd send them against an army of ogres and Fomorians. It would be a slaughter."

"Ogres and Fomorians? Did you see them?" Topaz spoke up at last.

"No, he must have kept them well back in the forest. Element of surprise and all. He's probably planning to bring them out tonight, so that when we look out the windows tomorrow morning, we'll be terrified. But his father's official terms mentioned them, and I don't doubt it. That news has been traveling across the land for days, and there have been many that have seen them. No, the only way we can win is if we simply hold out longer than they do."

Aunt Jilona declared, "It won't be the first time our family's weathered a siege in Swynmoor Castle, and it certainly won't be the last. Why, Malvern's great-grandfather --"

"With all due respect to my ancestors, I really don't have time to stand in the courtyard chatting about them. I've got to go over our food stores with Waltham to see how long we can reasonably hold out before we starve."

"Thank heavens we just received our pickle taxes for the year!" Glynis exclaimed.

"We'll certainly be eating a lot of them."

"I was about to tell you, before you rudely interrupted me," his Aunt Jilona interjected, "I've brought pound upon pound of dried sausages from Finbarr Springs. It's one of the local specialties there, and I wanted to share with you. They're positively divine with a bit of sharp cheese --"

"That does sound wonderful," his mother said.

"Thank you, Aunt Jilona. Every bit helps."

"I'd wanted it to be a surprise, but --"

"Yes, circumstances change. Really, I'd better be off. If we're going to be under siege, there are a lot of things that need to be prepared."

"I can help," Topaz said quietly, "Let me do something useful."

"Good heavens, dear, you mustn't do that! You'll spoil your dress! Come back into the parlor at once and work on your needlepoint," his aunt protested.

The tall girl cast a rueful glance after him as she was bustled back into the castle between the two older ladies. Tom watched the tail feathers of Aunt Jilona's stuffed bird bobbing up and down ridiculously on top of her head as she retreated.

Kerris rubbed her thumb, where a blister was beginning to form. At least she'd managed to find a pile of clean rags near the pantry, so that she could make some bandages. To make her overall discomfort worse, there was a storm brewing outside, and she'd always been like a living barometer. Even the most distantly approaching bad weather made the hairs on the back of her neck stand up and the muscles twinge all down her right side. Not that anyone else would have known that it was going to rain. The skies had remained deceptively clear as the future Earl of Swynmoor had ridden out to parlay with Reynaud the Black. That, of course, was related to a far bigger problem than any of her strictly physical ailments. And she'd missed it all!

Had she been watching out of a window, carefully recording what was happening for posterity, as she should have been? No, when she'd gone to get a good view, there had scarcely been enough time to notice the clear skies. Then suddenly, the cook had grabbed her by the ear, dragged her down into the kitchen, and forced her to peel a mountain of potatoes! Because the servant girls had all gone to the Harvest Ball, Kerris had found herself constantly pressed into service, practically since the moment she'd set foot in Swynmoor Castle. She'd been ordered around by the ancient cook, the equally ancient chamberlain, Lady Swynmoor's maid, and even the monks, who should have known better. They'd demanded that she fetch and carry for them, bring water from the well, sweep the floors, and now even peel potatoes!

It was outrageous. At Swynmoor Abbey, she'd worked on the pickles, like all the other Foundlings, but it was because they were the main source of income for the nuns. Everybody was expected to help with that important task, including the Abbess. The sisters, as well as the Foundling girls who would probably one day become nuns, were not expected to do common housework. There were lay servant girls to do those things for them. They received a modest amount of money for their labors, but the local farming families were glad to lend their daughters to the abbey for more important reasons. In exchange for their help, the nuns specifically included the girls in their prayers. This practically guaranteed that God would make sure that they got good husbands and led prosperous lives.

This highly satisfactory arrangement freed the sisters up for God's more important work. They translated and copied books -- more recent holy ones from other lands, as well as the mustier volumes that had been left over from Highreach's pagan past. In addition, the nuns brewed elixirs and dried herbs for medicines, and the villagers frequently turned to the abbey for help when a family member or even a farm animal was sick or injured. They also prayed frequently, clutching their holy beads and intervening against God's wrath several times during each day and night. Without their prayers, who would keep the crops from being blighted or the plague from descending upon Swynmoor? And yet, the first time she had ventured out from behind abbey walls, Kerris had been treated like a servant. No wonder Sister Goldrose had vowed never to go out into the world again.

At last, however, she had managed to free herself from the seemingly unending job of potato peeling. When the cook's back was turned, Kerris crept out of the kitchen before the old lady could give her anything else to do. Now she was sneaking around the halls of the castle on a holy mission -- to find a lamp or two with plenty of wick left, as well as a decent amount of oil. She planned to spirit these off the servant girls' room that she was temporarily occupying and get back to her true work. She had only one book to translate -- the Old Reachian text that she had inadvertently tucked into her pocket. But reading it would allow her to at least keep up with her studies somewhat while she was away. Why, she even had a dictionary to help her whenever she got stuck on a word! Perhaps the sisters were right -- God could be counted on to provide whatever you truly needed. Well, now she needed a source of light, and she was determined to make it as easy as possible for Him to give her one. She tried to open one of the many wooden doors that seemed to be almost randomly scattered along each side of the hallway. It was locked. Why did these nobles make it so difficult to find a lamp?

Kerris silently resolved that if she couldn't go back to the abbey soon, she would expand her exploration of the castle to see if she could discover a library. Rich folks like these usually had one, she thought, even though the sisters had told her that some nobles chose not to learn how to read. Imagine! Being so wealthy that you could afford to keep a well-stocked library in your own home, but never bothering to read any of the books! Meanwhile, the nuns had to use some of their precious pickle money or beg for donations in order to keep themselves supplied with even a moderate number of volumes. The very thought of it annoyed her so much that she forgot to pay attention to where she was going and stubbed her toe hard against a wall. Coupled with the increasing ache in her muscles, which was steadily working its way down her side from her right shoulder, the foot injury was too much.

"Owwaugh!" she cried out involuntarily, before she could stop herself.

She paused for a moment, not daring to move in case the cook, or someone else who had an unpleasant task for her, had noticed. Almost inevitably, a voice could be heard very faintly, as if the sound had to travel up a flight of stairs.

"Kerris!" it called, "Kerris Seaborn -- is that you? I know you're somewhere in this castle! You may think that you're too high and mighty to help in the kitchen, but --"

It was becoming louder, implying that the angry person was getting closer. Frantically, she began trying each of the doors in turn, desperately looking for a place to hide. At last, one of them gave way, and she muttered a few words of thanks to God. She then rushed into the previously concealed room and shut the door firmly behind her. It was windowless and very tiny. Squinting into the dimly lit space, she saw that it contained buckets, mops, brooms and other things that were useful for cleaning. She sighed, hunkering down in the near-darkness to wait until the threat had passed. It wasn't her ideal hiding spot, of course, but she would take what she could get. The voice shrilly calling her name grew louder, as her pursuer's footsteps got closer to the place where she was concealed. She held her breath, trying to make as little noise as possible. For a long moment, her potential tormentor actually seemed to pause in front of the broom closet, but shortly after that, the footsteps receded down the hallway. She let out a long sigh of relief.

Kerris remained where she was for several minutes after that, making sure that the cook, the chamberlain, or whoever was looking for her had truly given up. Just as she was thinking of beginning her search for light anew, she realized that the foot she had already hurt was now asleep. Painfully, she wriggled her toes in her squatting position, trying to restore at least some circulation. Without any warning, and much to her astonishment, the closet door was flung open. Light briefly flooded in. Certain she had been caught after all, she cried out, raising her arm across her face to shield her eyes from the brightness. Just as suddenly, however, the darkness returned again, but now someone was on her side of the door! There really was very little space. A knobby knee brushed up against her forehead.

"Who --" she began.

A man's voice whispered, "I'm frightfully sorry to ask this, but could you please be quiet? My Aunt Jilona is looking for me, and I need a place to hide."

Silently, she nodded. Whoever it was, she certainly knew how he felt. Something about this castle seemed to inspire the need for concealment. The man dropped down, lowering himself into a crouch beside her. It was a slight improvement from having his knee menacing her face, but still, his shoulder was now far too close to her nose. She gagged as quietly as possible as the sickly sweet smell of mothballs filled her nostrils. As her eyes readjusted to the very dim lighting, she began to make out some features of the person who was now uncomfortably near to her. This was not the first time she had seen him. Before she could really work out who he was, though, the sound of many tiny dogs barking shrilly interrupted her thoughts. As the yapping got closer, it was accompanied by the scratching sounds of hundreds of little dog toenails on a stone floor.

An irritated female voice called out, "Toooomlin! Tomlin, you good-for-nothing, where have you gone?"

At that moment, the absurdity of the situation struck Kerris, and she barely managed to suppress a giggle. She stole a glance at the young man beside her, who was apparently called Tomlin, and noticed that he was struggling not to burst out laughing himself. At last, however, the voice of the man's aunt grew fainter as she continued down the hallway, accompanied by her pack of dogs. At last, when it seemed far enough away, the two of them gave in to their baser instincts and began to laugh almost uncontrollably.

"So, who was after you?" he asked, at last.

"The cook, I think. But I'm not entirely sure. Old people often sound alike to me."

"I never thought of that, but I suppose you're right. I say -- I know it's rather unpleasant, but would you mind staying put for a few more minutes? I want to be sure that she doesn't decide to come back this way any time soon."

Kerris nodded, then decided that if she was going to be stuck in a closet with this young man, she might as well get as good a look at him as possible. As her eyes adjusted still further to the dimness inside the closet, she became aware that his reeking clothes were decorated ostentatiously with medals and emblems that clinked together quietly in the dark. As she was able to make out more of his facial features, she realized that he had been at that dinner the night before. He was one of the rich people who had been so terribly rude to her! The nerve of him, squeezing into her hiding place like this, after how he'd treated her! Her shoulder twinged particularly painfully, increasing her overall irritation.

"I know who you are!" she whispered fiercely, "You're Lord Tomlin -- one of the nobles who wouldn't let me make my speech!"

He sputtered quietly, "Good heavens -- you're that girl from the abbey! The lovely one with the honey-colored hair! I couldn't -- I mean, I didn't see who you --"

"My name is Kerris Seaborn," she said a bit haughtily, "Not that it would matter to you."

"Why that's --" he replied, fumbling for the right words, "Well, nothing could be further from the truth!"

"Why would you care what I'm called? So you can know what name to shout as you order me to fetch and carry for you?"

"I'd never --" he began.

"Oh, really? And I suppose that you don't know that everyone from the chamberlain to your aunt's maid has been shouting at me since I arrived, making me do housework?"

"Look -- Kerris -- I truly don't know what's been happening to you. I mean no offense, but I've had quite a lot of troubles of my own! I've been very busy --"

"Doing what, my lord?" she asked sarcastically, "Counting your money?"

"Please don't address me like that. When you say 'my lord', it sounds positively horrid. I'd much rather that you just call me Tom. And if you think I've any gold coins to count, you really do have the wrong idea about me. All the wealth in the family belongs to my Aunt Jilona -- you know, the woman who was just shouting my name in the hallway, accompanied by the roving kennel?"

"Why are you hiding from her, anyway?" she asked, slightly less skeptical.

"Honestly, I've been trying to avoid being married off by my aunt to a woman that I seriously think might have a giant as a distant ancestor."

"That isn't very nice," said Kerris, trying not to sound amused.

"Perhaps not, but it's true. Aunt Jilona is stalking the halls like a resident ghost, trying to track me down, so that I can play croquet or some other nonsense with this girl. Meanwhile, I need to take an inventory of all the food in the castle."

"Why?"

"So that I can get at least some idea of how long we can withstand a siege from the army of ogres and Fomorians that's camping on our doorstep."

"Well -- I could do the inventory for you."

"You can do accounts?" he asked, sounding genuinely surprised, "But you're a girl!"

The icy coldness returned to her voice.

"I've lived in an abbey with nuns my entire life, where men are forbidden to enter. Who do you think inventories our food at the end of each harvest season? And do you think the faeries keep track of how many barrels of pickles we've made?"

"Forgive me -- I didn't mean to offend you! It's just that I've never met a girl before who was taught to do sums. I'm sure things must be very different for you, since you've been brought up by the sisters."

"Yes," she said, noticeably less hostilely, "I've never been away from the abbey before in my life. I was terribly excited to see something of the world. But ever since I've been here, I've just wanted to go home."

"Why on earth would you want to do that? Life at the abbey must be terribly dull."

"At least I don't do servants' work there. I study. I write out translations of old books. I pray and help the sisters tend to the sick. And sometimes, yes, I help them with their accounts. Today, however -- I performed the rewarding tasks of fetching buckets of water from the well and peeling potatoes."

And I'm in agony because it's going to rain, she added silently, not wanting to explain her sensitivity to storms. Even though it was nothing more than a natural phenomenon, she worried that it might make her sound like a witch to Tom. Briefly, she wondered why she cared at all about what he thought of her, but she dismissed the idea without too much examination. Rich folks had a lot of power, and possibly being considered a witch could be a dangerous thing.

"I really am dreadfully sorry. Listen -- why don't I have a word with Waltham, our chamberlain. I'll tell him that from now on, you're to do more important things -- like taking an inventory of our food stores. And if you want to carry on with translating books, you can help yourself to anything you'd like from the library. What do you say?"

"That sounds wonderful! But, I have two conditions."

"Yes?"

"I'd like some lamps and lamp oil."

"Done. What's the second?"

"I want to get out of this closet. No offense, but your clothes smell powerfully of mothballs."

For the first time in several days, Tom had a really good laugh. As if to warn him against being in too good of a mood, however, thunder began to rumble ominously in the distance. The hairs on Kerris' neck stood at full attention, and the muscles in her shoulder stabbed at her pitilessly.

Naturally, there was thunder in the air. A really big storm would be all they needed, Reynaud thought. That would take the entire metaphorical pile of pig manure that this pathetic attempt at making camp had become and just throw the final stinking shovelful on top. He pressed the thumb and middle finger of his right hand to both of his temples at the same time, encircling his own forehead with his hand. He squeezed his eyes shut, allowing himself to fervently wish, just for a second or two, that he was somewhere -- anywhere -- else. Opening his eyes and returning his hand to his side, he addressed Garrok, the ogres' general, as calmly as he could.

"So -- let me see if I understand what happened. The ogres got tired of the Fomorians calling them women."

"Yes, they angered us."

"Your men decided that, to punish them, you weren't going to cook for them anymore."

"We did," the ogre said, thrusting his bottom tusks forward in a grin.

"So before we broke camp this morning, to get back at the Fomorians, you allowed your soldiers to throw all of our frying pans, pots, spoons, ladles, kettles and other cooking things into the river."

"Yes," Garrok agreed, grinning even more widely.

"And they all washed away, as far as you know, into the ocean."

"The Fomorians will be sorry now!"

"Ah," he sighed.

The ogre continued to gaze at him, beaming, as if he was waiting for the human to tell him how clever he'd been. It almost pained Reynaud to let him down. Almost.

"You realize that those were the only things that any of us had to cook our dinners in?"

The ogre nodded.

"And because the Fomorians were insulting you, I made them set up the tents up tonight while the ogres got the food for our dinners."

"Yes! We speared many fish! We will have plenty to eat tonight! No one will go hungry! The Fomorians will see!"

"Ogres don't eat raw fish, right?"

Garrok spat onto the ground in disgust.

"Raw fish? Ugh -- that is only for animals!"

"How do you think that you are going to cook the fish?"

"We have many jars of oil! We will fry the fish and have a feast fit for the gods!"

"What a lot of 'f''s you've managed to pack into that sentence. Let me try again. What are you going to put the oil into to fry the fish?"

He looked at Reynaud as if he feared that the human might be a little mentally deficient.

"Frying pans. How else would we make fried fish?"

"The ones that you threw into the river this morning?"

"The ones that we --"

The ogre stopped, mid-sentence. The black knight watched as comprehension slowly and incrementally stole across Garrok's expression.

"The frying pans! Oh! But -- how will we make our fried fish of the gods?"

"Yes. You see, when you threw out the cooking things, you hurt everybody -- not just the Fomorians."

"But -- the fried fish!"

"Look, for tonight, we'll have our fish cooked on sticks over the fire. In the morning, we can send a raiding party into the village for cooking supplies."

Garrok spat again.

"I spit on the Fomorians! Because of them, we cannot have fried fish!"

"But it was the ogres who threw the pans into the river."

"It is their fault! They are the sons of goats and women!"

Reynaud sighed. The time had come to pick his battles, and he didn't choose this one.

"Be that as it may. Please go back to your soldiers and tell them to fashion sticks for cooking fish over the fire pits. I'm sure that they are already quite hungry."

"As you will," Garrok said resentfully.

As if he considered the lack of fried fish his Commander's fault, as well as the Fomorians', he rapidly turned on his heel to return to his troop of ogres. Far before he was out of earshot, Garrok began grumbling murderously under his breath. Reynaud was doing some muttering himself as he began to walk back toward the place where his tent was loudly being set up. The Fomorians had insisted on putting it in the direct center of all of the army's tents. Because that wouldn't be one of the first places that his enemies would think to look, he mused, sardonically. His black tent would stand out in the middle of the garishly colored ones of the ogres and Fomorians like a dark bullseye, complete with a flapping hedgehog flag on top to draw the eye. He'd tried to explain why this configuration was a terrible idea, but the Fomorians had insisted that the placement was their way of honoring him as a Commander. With each passing day, he was beginning to feel increasingly as if he was not moving at the head of an army, but instead was traveling as a part of some itinerant circus, complete with the brightly colored tents of the clowns.

Just to make things worse, he knew that tomorrow's raid on the village would inspire laughter, rather than fear, in the hearts of his enemies, as surely as the hedgehog flag had always done. Swynmoor had certainly been right about that, Reynaud thought bitterly. His family crest had always been a source of embarrassment for him. And now people would hear about his dread army of ogres and Fomorians breaking down doors in the village, momentarily terrifying the women and children before making off with -- their pots and pans. Of course, his family would eventually receive news of the kitchen raid, and he was sure that he'd be able to hear his brothers' laughter all the way from Fynchester. He stopped gloomily outside of the mostly constructed black tent with the humiliating hedgehog banner. Unsettlingly, he realized that he was hearing a lot of squelching noises from under his feet. He looked down to see that his boots were already buried in mud past his ankles. This was not a good sign. The first drops of rain began to fall, as thunder rumbled ominously in the distance once again.

3

Claiming a headache, Topaz managed a strategic retreat to the place that served as her bedroom at Swynmoor Castle. If she hadn't gotten away from the intense scrutiny of Tomlin's aunt and mother soon, she would have had no choice but to simply go mad. Throwing her embroidery in a heap onto her dresser, she sat down heavily on her bed and tried to resist having a good cry. Tears would mar the makeup that Lady Swynmoor's maid had spent more than an hour applying that morning. She couldn't loosen her corset without help, but at least she could kick off the ridiculously frilly shoes that pinched her feet with every step. Of course, they had narrow heels because that style was de rigueur this year, but she couldn't imagine anyone who needed them less than she did. Why did the queen, who set the fashions, have to be so short? Topaz already towered over all of the eligible men in Highreach.

Just thinking of the phrase "eligible men" conjured up a mental image of Tomlin's disdainful face. Like every other potential husband she'd been introduced to, he was, at best, utterly indifferent to her. It didn't matter that she was able to play the harp better than most young ladies of quality. She could also keep up her end of the pleasant banter that was expected of girls in the marriage market, as well as embroider respectably, ride a horse sidesaddle, and manage even the most complicated steps of all the latest dances. Her complexion was quite good, and her hair was a color that was considered fashionable this year. Of course, none of it mattered. She was simply too tall, and her height would probably condemn her to a lifetime of childless spinsterhood. This was her third season since she had come out as debutante, and much to her mother's chagrin, ladies were beginning to whisper pityingly behind their fans when Topaz entered a room.

There had been a time when her height hadn't been a source of misery for her, even though she'd been taller than all of her cousins as a little girl.

Her father had gently chucked her under the chin and given her shiny silver coins to spend on sweets when she'd been in the nursery, calling her his "big girl". Admittedly, her nanny had always laughed a bit nervously when the subject of height had come up. However, the old woman assured her anxious mother that many young girls went through an early "growth spurt", and it just meant that Topaz wouldn't get much taller after she went to finishing school. Unfortunately, however, she'd continued to grow several inches each year while she was away. The other girls began to tease her about it, and the headmistress became concerned that such a tall young lady might have difficulties with procuring a husband. Growing more desperate with each passing year, she inflicted a series of increasingly terrible remedies on the unfortunate girl.

Each night, Topaz was forced to sleep with several books tied onto the top of her head to "weigh her down". This plainly failed to work, and she grew another six inches over the course of four months. She was then compelled to stand in her stocking feet in a bucket of freezing water for an hour after supper each day, in the hopes that her bones and muscles would contract from the cold. When this, also, did not stop her from growing, a specialist was summoned, who insisted on daily copious bloodletting from the balls of her feet. Although this made walking quite painful, the bleeding had no other effect. The specialist soon left the school grounds in a huff, offended that Topaz continued to grow, despite his ministrations. When she graduated and returned home, she was not only taller than all the women in her family, but the men, as well. Her previously doting father, who hadn't seen her for many years, could not conceal his dismay when she joined the adults for dinner for the first time.

"Well, you certainly did turn out to be a very big girl indeed," he said.

The mortified nanny, despite having become somewhat decrepit, was cruelly dismissed from the family's service. Topaz thought that perhaps it was superstitiously feared that she might bring other little girls up to be embarrassingly tall. And initially, there had been some discussion among the older aunts about whether young Topaz would be allowed to make her debut, after all. In the end, it was decided that the Stonemonts' pride could withstand a few pointed comments about the height of one of their own. A very skilled seamstress was summoned to the house and instructed to work any wonders with color and fabric that she could. It was somewhat vainly hoped that she might be able to distract people from the fact that the girl who was wearing these glamorous confections would be far taller than any of the men that she was supposed to attract.

Like other girls from noble families, her debut had commenced in Highholde, where one of her aunts had formally presented her to the king and queen. As she'd waited her turn to approach the throne, there had been some snickering and murmuring among the courtiers, but nothing more than she'd feared. At last, her name was announced, and Topaz had stepped forward to make her first official curtsey to the royal family. Just as she'd begun to hope that everything might come off without too much embarrassment, the three-year-old princess, who was sitting in a tiny, ornate chair next to her mother, removed a thumb from her mouth to point at Topaz.

"Mama, is that lady a giant?" she asked.

The acoustics in the throne room were, of course, excellent, since a previous king had wanted to make very sure that when he spoke, everyone would hear. The princess' words carried. As the queen hurried to shush her little daughter, Topaz felt her face beginning to flush hot with embarrassment. One of the powdered nobles let loose with a particularly obnoxious, tittering laugh that he'd apparently been struggling to suppress. Courtier after courtier began to chuckle, then chortle, until they finally gave way to all out whooping, howling merriment. Before she could kiss the queen's ring, her aunt grabbed onto her by the elbow and practically dragged her out by the nearest exit. This door happened to lead to a long corridor that servants used to bring hors d'oeuvres on silver trays and goblets of wine into the throne room. Humiliatingly, her enormous puffed sleeve caught the edge of a platter, and the little jewel-like shrimps that had been delicately arranged on it went flying through the air, spilling onto the ornate carpet.

"I'm sorry -- so sorry!" she called back over her shoulder, as her aunt resolutely pulled her along, seeming oblivious to the servant's distress.

Despite this initial disaster, her family had insisted that she stay in Highholde for the rest of the season. After all, they had spent considerable sums on the clothing and jewelry for her debut, and they certainly didn't intend to waste it just because she'd managed to embarrass herself. She was forced to endure several months of teas, operas, banquets, and balls, during which people, especially the other debutantes, openly laughed at her and cruelly referred to her as "The Giantess". The balls, of course, were the worst. While the other girls whirled through the minuets, pavanes, and quadrilles with an ever-changing series of dance partners, Topaz sat by the wall with the chaperones, her dance card empty. Inevitably, she ended up drinking endless glasses of punch and praying for the evening to be over, so that she could cry in private about not being asked to dance by anyone again.

The irony of it all was that, had anyone invited her to take part, she could have done so with more grace than most of the other women at the ball. She had learned all of the popular dances at school, and the teacher had often complimented Topaz about her natural talent for remembering even the most complicated choreography. While her fellow students were bumping into each other and squealing with laughter, she had effortlessly turned and curtseyed through the most difficult steps. Unfortunately, none of the men would ever give her the opportunity to exhibit her skills. Afraid of looking short by comparison, they chose even the clumsiest of debutantes over her.

At last, when she'd been through several seasons of such humiliations, her mother had summoned the seamstress once again. This time, she was commissioned to make Topaz some alluring, yet still respectable, bathing costumes. Expressing a firm desire to take the waters, her mother then bundled the hopelessly tall girl off to accompany her to Finbarr Springs. At least there would be no embarrassing dances. Topaz wore flat seaside shoes and spent most of her time sitting under her parasol on the beaches, or better still, up to her neck in water at the natural hot springs. Perhaps if she wasn't always looming over everyone, her mother told her, some appropriate man might find her compelling. Unfortunately, this approach did not work any better. Most of the things that women did at Finbarr springs to attract men also involved standing next to them, such as long games of croquet. To her horror, she found that playing this game required her to have a special mallet made that was suitable for her extraordinary height. Its handle stuck up among the others like an ostrich poking its head out above a group of pheasants. Archery contests were also popular among the debutantes, and she was quite competent at the sport. However, it involved a lot of standing around beside other ladies to wait for her turn, which inevitably invited comment from onlookers about how she positively towered over them.

Her mother had nearly cried with relief when her friend, Jilona, had offered to take Topaz to Swynmoor Castle and introduce her to her unmarried nephew, Tomlin. And for a time, at least, the tall girl had begun to hope that, with such a direct attempt at matchmaking, she might actually manage to get a husband, after all. Of course, the nephew in question thought that her height was positively hilarious, as all of the other bachelors at court and Finbarr Springs had done. It wasn't even as if she was being particularly choosy, she thought bitterly, tossing one of the paste stars that had fallen out of her hair onto the floor. She would have happily married a fat man, or a widower that was much older than she was. But even men like these, who had obvious roadblocks to finding marital happiness, scorned her. And that smug Lord Tomlin was the worst of all! Very well then, as soon as this siege was over, she would ask Lady Swynmoor if she could go home -- even beg her, if necessary. She didn't want to spend one day more than she had to being an object of ridicule. Perhaps she would buy a few of those little dogs that the older woman favored, since she would apparently need the company in her lonely spinsterhood. She picked up her embroidery and began to sew, determined not to think about Tomlin.

After an hour or two, there was a knock at the door, and she opened it to find that Lady Swynmoor's maid had arrived to help her change for dinner. The girl opened the wardrobe, suggesting a few options for dresses that were suitable for the evening. Topaz sighed and told her to choose whatever she liked best. It didn't matter. Nothing that she could possibly put on would ever make Tomlin, or any other man, find her attractive. She was simply too tall. Accordingly, the maid chose a fussy gown in bright purple, then began the arduous task of redoing her hair and makeup to match. It took a very long time, of course, but at last, she was ready to join the family for supper. She wondered if the food would be any good, since of course, the company would not be. Not that she had anything against Lady Swynmoor or her considerably quieter sister-in-law, but she had no common history with either of them. There was only so long that it was bearable to make small talk, especially when it had become obvious that the young man you had traveled so far to meet wanted nothing to do with you.

Topaz was the second one to arrive at the table, after Lady Glynis. The two of them sat there for a while, sipping wine and waiting for the others to join them. Since there were so few servants at the castle, the meals had become decidedly informal. All of the covered platters had simply been left on the table, their contents steaming under them, allowing the nobles to serve themselves. Topaz didn't mind. It was something of a relief not to have to wait for the servants to bring all of the courses around to everyone. Even though she could hear her mother in her mind, scolding her for rudeness, she curiously reached over and uncovered a rather small dish that had been left near her elbow. It was pickled red peppers. They smelled delicious, and she had always been fond of spicy things. Surreptitiously, as Lady Glynis was reaching under the table to pet one of her sister-in-law's ubiquitous dogs, she spooned a pepper into her hand, raised it to her mouth, and crunched into it. It was delicious, and its piquant heat made her tongue tingle pleasantly.

Raising her eyes to make sure that the other woman was still busy with the animal, she spooned another two into her hand. Even if she was caught, she reflected, it truly didn't matter anymore. She had only come here because she'd thought that she would be meeting a man who could potentially become her husband. He plainly wasn't interested, so she had very little need to impress his mother with her table manners. She popped the other pickled peppers into her mouth simultaneously and chewed. They really were fantastic. At last, Lady Swynmoor and Tomlin were making their way into the dining room, accompanied by many more little dogs. The older woman was scolding him about something before they even sat down.

"Well, now that we're all here, let us say grace, shall we?" interrupted Tomlin's mother.

Lady Swynmoor added, "Yes, Tomlin, you should do the honors. You're the official head of the household while your Uncle Malvern is away, after all."

"Oh, very well," he sighed.

The four of them put their thumbs and forefingers together and closed their eyes.

"Dear God," he began, "Protect us in our time of need, when we are being besieged by our enemies."

Topaz suddenly had the extremely unsettling sensation that she was growing taller by the moment. She rolled her eyes at her own foolishness. She'd obviously become so paranoid about her own height that she was now imagining things about it.

"And bless our food, as we come together --"

No, it really did feel like she was getting taller. She opened her eyes, and her plate actually seemed further away from her face than it had been when she'd first joined Lady Glynis. She didn't want to interrupt Lord Tomlin when he was praying, but her corset stays were straining and breaking, one by one. She needed to hurry back to her room before something terribly embarrassing happened. She had just made up her mind to excuse herself from the table when, with a crack like thunder, her chair gave way under her weight. The other three people opened their eyes to see a somewhat larger version of Topaz on the floor in a confused pile of purple ruffles, the broken fragments of her wooden seat on the ground next to her. Several of the tiny dogs hurried over to sniff at her, as the others began barking shrilly to let people know that something startling had happened.

"Good heavens!" exclaimed Lady Swynmoor.

"I say --" began Tom.

The threads on her dress were decidedly coming free by the second. Just that moment, her delicate shoes burst apart, leaving her feet exposed in her rapidly ripping stockings.

"Forgive me," she said, awkwardly holding what remained of her dress over her bosom, "I really cannot stay for supper!"

While she still had some clothing left, she ran out, feeling like a dreadful parody of herself when she'd had to flee the throne room. She was being obliged to duck out of places far too often for her own liking, let alone her relatives'. Rushing down the corridors, she realized that, in her distress, she hadn't been too particular about where she was headed. She had no idea where her room was, and all of the hallways and doors looked the same to her. She was hopelessly lost, shedding more fabric by the minute, and still continuing to grow. Her head was only inches from the ceiling now. If there had been any servants going about their business in the halls, they would have been staring after her curiously.

Her impending nakedness made her desperate, and she began trying to open doors at random. They all seemed to be locked. Tiny jewels began to pop off of the bodice of her gown, leaving a glittering trail behind her. At last, one door opened when she pulled on its handle, revealing only a nondescript staircase. Without as much as a pause for breath, she began to descend, going down and further down still, into the bowels of Swynmoor Castle. She had to duck down to avoid scraping the top of her head on the ceiling as she fled. Each of her stockings in turn ripped from her toes to her garters, which also broke apart, shedding delicate lace and gold dust. She was truly barefoot, not to mention bare-legged, now. At the bottom of the stairs, she found another door and flung it open, as the last remnants of her clothing fell to the floor. Thinking that she'd found a place to hide just in time, she stepped through the archway without looking where she was going. As the door swung shut behind her with a terrible, clanking finality, she saw the night sky and felt grass under her feet. She was outside.

"No!" she cried.

Topaz turned and tried to push the door open again, since there was no handle on the outside to pull on. With a lurching feeling in the pit of her stomach, she realized that it had locked behind her. On the balance, it was probably for the best that she had made her way out, since she was rapidly growing too big to fit in even the most generously sized room of the castle. However, she was enormous, stark naked, and trapped outside in the dark. Just to make things worse, it would probably be cold and damp soon, as the weather had been for the past few nights. Thoroughly mortified, she was certain that this episode would surely finish off even the tiniest possibility she'd had left of ever getting married. Respectable young ladies simply did not go gallivanting around the countryside without a stitch on, even if they had unexpectedly grown to gigantic proportions. And she might never go back to being a normal size again -- if the height she'd previously been could even be considered "normal", she thought ruefully.

She felt her eyes welling up with massive tears, but she managed to choke them back just before they fell. It was all too horrible. She didn't really even know where she was, let alone in which direction she wanted to go. Wiping at her eyes, she took a few deep breaths. As she looked around to take in her surroundings, it became apparent that she'd gone out some sort of secret back door. Moments after she'd emerged, it had blended in with the rest of the wall behind her. It was so perfectly concealed, if she hadn't just come out of it, she wouldn't have believed that it was there. She suspected that some sort of magic spell had been used on it when the castle had been built, centuries ago. Yes, she was definitely at the back of Swynmoor Castle. She briefly considered running into the woods to hide, ideally never to be seen again, but that wasn't a sensible course of action. She wasn't like one of those wild girls in the ballads who could live merrily in the forest, cooking wild game over open fires. She was decent at archery, but she had only shot targets before, and she didn't possess even the most basic of cooking or gardening skills. No, as painful as it was to admit it, she would simply have to find people again if she was ever going to get out of this mess.

So -- going back into the castle wasn't an option, and there was nothing directly ahead of her but trees. It seemed best to go around to the front of the castle and find the road that she had traveled on when she'd arrived. She would also have to convince some kindly soul to aid her, though she wasn't entirely sure how to go about that, especially at her current size. Perhaps Lady Swynmoor or Lady Glynis would see her from a window. They might be able to summon a priest who had knowledge of an alchemical spell that could shrink her back down. Of course, it was just as likely that she would be seen by Lord Tomlin, but that possibility was too terrible to contemplate. As she started walking, she realized that she seemed to have stopped growing. The ground wasn't getting any further away as she looked down at it. Taking stock of her new size, she noticed that she was about half as tall as the castle itself. She tried to move as quietly as possible, but each footstep seemed to resonate with a booming sound. It took remarkably few strides for her to reach the other side of Swynmoor Castle, where the drawbridge and gates were located. Just down the hill, she could see what looked like an entire village of tents in various sizes. It had to be the encampment of Reynaud the Black and his army. Perhaps someone there would take pity on her, she thought. It wasn't her family that the Fynchesters seemed to have a grudge against, after all.

She began to make her way toward the tents, but a terrible thought crept into her mind like a spider. All she wanted was to go home, to get away from Lord Tomlin, who disliked her and was probably laughing about her unhappiness right now. The only reason she'd had to stay on in this castle, where she plainly wasn't wanted, was because this man and his army had blocked her in. Why, if she'd been able to go home, perhaps this ridiculous growth spurt would never have happened at all! She wasn't sure what had brought it on, but it probably had something to do with being here. After all, she'd always been very tall, but since she'd arrived here, she'd become a full-blown giant. With each step she grew more resentful. Stupid siege! Stupid army! Now she was enormous, and it was all their fault!

Before she fully realized what she was doing, she'd angrily brought one of her colossal feet down on one of the tents, smashing it. Flailing around, several ogres disentangled themselves from the flattened fabric and rushed out into the night. They stopped to stare up at Topaz, seemingly frozen with astonishment. She looked at the crushed tent under her foot, feeling a strange sort of satisfaction, but it wasn't enough to fully slake her long pent-up fury. She kicked at another one, overturning it and sending its shouting occupants running for cover. The tears that she'd managed to hold back twice today began to fall, splashing the mercenaries like huge, salty raindrops. She brought her foot down on a third tent, heedless of the cries of the ogres and Fomorians.

"Stupid tents! Stupid army!" she sobbed hysterically, "I just want to go home!"

From inside his black pavilion, where he was poring over his maps and books of strategy, Reynaud heard a terrible commotion. He waited a moment or two to see if it would die down. It was probably the Fomorians and ogres getting into a brawl over something ridiculous again. Perhaps, for once, they would manage to work it out on their own. Unfortunately, the noise continued, so he emerged from his tent to find out what the trouble was, this time. What he saw was perhaps the most extraordinary thing he'd ever beheld. A positively immense, though still strangely beautiful, naked young woman was weeping and stomping on the encampment with her lovely, massive feet. Despite her size, she was definitely not a giant. Every giant he'd heard of or read about was dark green and hideous. This extraordinary creature's pale skin shone like snow in the moonlight. He instinctively understood that this creature was just a girl -- an enormous and apparently very unhappy one -- but a girl nonetheless. He looked up, unable to do anything but stare. Izir and Garrok hurried over to his side.

"Commander, we are under attack by a giant!" announced the ogre.

"He see that! Fomorians get ready the cannons!" Izir added.

He blinked and shook his head to clear it.

"Cannons? No -- absolutely not! No cannons."

"You want us to fight the giant off with arrows? It would be --"

"No! No cannons, no arrows!" shouted Reynaud, "Hold your fire. That is no giant -- that is a woman!"

The generals looked doubtful.

"That -- woman?" asked the Fomorian.

"Yes, she's just a girl, really, poor thing. I'm going to see if I can help her."

Reynaud whistled for his dark horse, Altairos, who had been grazing nearby. He came charging over immediately, only stopping for his owner to leap skillfully onto his back.

"Remember," he shouted from the back of the horse, "Do not attack her! Hold your fire at all costs!"

The two generals shrugged and looked at each other, equally at a loss. Nonetheless, they knew what they'd been commanded to do and trusted that the human had a plan, however misguided it might be. They made their way over to their black bicorns and also began riding through the camp, crying out the Commander's message to their men.

"Do not attack! Hold your fire!" they shouted from their mounts, as their men looked at them in astonishment.

Riding boldly toward the colossal woman, who was continuing to sob and destroy tents, Reynaud found himself wishing that his horse hadn't already been unsaddled for the evening. If he'd had stirrups to stand up in, he would have done so. As it was, he had to make do with calling up to her as loudly as possible while sitting bareback on his horse.

"I say, madam! Can I be of any assistance?" he shouted, as gallantly as he could.

She stopped extremely suddenly, a leg still raised in midair. Turning her tear-streaked gaze downward, she looked directly at him, her vast facial features arranged in a startled expression.

"What did you say?" she asked.

She put her foot down carefully, so that it didn't do any more damage. He cleared his throat and tried again.

"I asked if there was anything I could do to help. You seem -- well -- rather upset."

She blinked once or twice, then began crying even more violently than before. What little was left of her makeup and powder ran down her face in streaks.

"You want to help me?" she asked, between great, gulping sobs.

"Er, yes," he answered, "If you'll tell me what I can do for you."

He tried to maneuver Altairos around so that they didn't get drenched with enormous tears, but they got hit with one or two, nonetheless. The horse shook his mane and looked at the girl resentfully. Truly weeping uncontrollably, she sat on the ground with an enormous thud, luckily only crushing a few of the tents that had already been vacated with one thigh. Her massive backside landed on a swathe of uninterrupted grass.

"I was in the castle, and --" she gulped.

As she haltingly told her story, something astounding happened. The girl began shrinking before his eyes, getting smaller and smaller until she was the size of a very tall, but still reasonably sized, human being. Reynaud found her even lovelier. He felt the urge to reach out and stroke her cheek to comfort her. Sensibly, however, he held back because it would have been terribly inappropriate, especially given her lack of clothing. He dismounted from his horse and moved closer to her on foot, wishing that he had a cloak to cover her nakedness.

"I'm going to take you back to my tent and find something for you to wear, all right? Please don't be afraid. I really don't mean you any harm."

She nodded, barely able to speak through her tears. As gently as possible, he picked her up and placed her on the back of Altairos, who whickered gently. Then, blushing with the terrible impropriety of it all, he mounted the horse behind her and put his arms around her waist. He was afraid that she'd grown so weak with crying, not to mention changing sizes, that she might fall off if he didn't hold onto her, no matter how slowly he told the horse to go. Much to their mutual embarrassment, they were cheered all the way back to his dark pavilion by what seemed like the entire army of Fomorians and ogres. They were very impressed with how skillfully their Commander had managed to halt the attack. He, in turn, was impressed they refrained from whistling and catcalling, as his brothers would surely have done. Also, not one of them was calling for any sort of violence to be done to her in retaliation. Perhaps he'd have to revise his opinions about his troops somewhat, after all.

The black horse delicately picked his way back through the tents, most of which Reynaud was pleased to note were still standing. Soon, they arrived at one with a hedgehog flag flying on top. He dismounted, patted Altairos, then helped the girl down with as little awkwardness as he could manage. As if he'd anticipated the need, Reynaud's manservant, Jack, appeared to take the horse back to his pasture to graze and sleep. Now unencumbered, the black haired young man pulled back his tent flap and gestured for her to come inside.

Although he did not travel as luxuriously as his father preferred, Reynaud's home away from home was far from a common soldier's. There was a brazier in the center of it with a warmly burning fire to keep the chill away. His bed, however hastily assembled, was a real bed with a headboard, pillows and fur covers. A clothes chest with an elaborately carved letter "F" on the lid sat at its foot, and there was a full-length mirror in a wooden frame next to it. A large table had been set up in one corner, which was covered in maps, books, and what looked to Topaz like a child's scattered toy soldiers. There was also another, smaller table, which held food and drink and had four chairs placed around it. Several candles burned in their sconces, so there was plenty of light. There were rugs on the floor with patterns that looked of Eastern origin, but mud had been so copiously tracked over them that it was difficult to tell what the weavers had originally intended for them to look like.

Reynaud immediately went over to the clothes chest and tossed a dark pair of his breeches and a shirt at the girl, who caught them. With a look of gratitude, she immediately began to clothe herself.

"All black I'm afraid," he said, "Not cheerful enough for a young woman like you, but father insists that I must keep up appearances. Strike fear into the hearts of my enemies and all that rubbish. Though why I'd seem a great deal less terrifying in green, I couldn't tell you."

"Thank you," she said, pulling the shirt over her head, "I actually prefer dark colors, but I haven't been allowed to wear them for a few years.

Not in fashion, you know."

He laughed, "It seems that both of us get little choice in our own clothing, then. How wonderful it is to be young and under other people's control. I'm sorry if the pants and sleeves on the shirt are a bit long for you. I wasn't exactly expecting --"

"A gigantic naked woman to drop in on you this evening? No, I don't suppose you would have been. And as you see, the length of your clothing works quite well for me. You've been too polite to mention it, but surely you've seen that even at my normal size, I'm rather absurdly tall. I could use a belt, though, if you have one to spare, since the waist on the pants is --"

She held the waistband out, showing him that there were many inches of fabric that she didn't need around her middle.

"Made for a man! A belt! Of course -- why didn't I think of that?"

Red with embarrassment once again, he scrambled over to the clothes chest and fumbled around in it. At last, he found his spare belt, which was inevitably made of black leather. He tossed it to her, and she cinched the pants in so that they would not fall down around her ankles.

"I'm sorry to trouble you like this, especially after I've behaved so badly," she said, "By all rights, you should probably throw me into a pit. Not that I should be giving you ideas, I suppose."

"My dear lady, I felt sorry for you from the first moment I laid eyes on you. After all, it's quite unusual for someone who's intent on viciously attacking an enemy encampment to be positively sobbing her eyes out. Which reminds me --"

He took a lace-edged dark handkerchief from a pocket, immersed it in the bowl of hand-washing water that was on the dining table, wrung it out slightly, and handed it to her.

"Perhaps you'd like to wash your face."

"Merciful angels -- my makeup! Not only giant-sized and naked but also looking like some sort of drowned ghost. Mother would be horrified!"

She rushed over to the mirror to clean off the ruined powder and makeup. Then, tut-tutting over her flyaway hair, she took the combs and pins out of it, allowing it to flow freely in a dark brown wave almost to her waist. She turned back to him when she was finished, looking fresh-faced and pretty. In his clothes, she seemed to Reynaud like a girl from one of those comedy plays that had been so popular back home. They were the sort in which it was integral to the plot for characters to run around pretending to be the opposite gender for one reason or another, when they obviously weren't. He gestured toward the dining table.

"Could I offer you some food or some wine, perhaps?" he asked, "It's simple fare, but --"

"Honestly, I'm absolutely ravenous. I had to run off before I had any supper because I started growing."

"Then, by all means, sit down. There's more than I could ever eat here."

The two of them sat at the little table, and Reynaud served each of them a large ladle-full of fish stew, a chunk of only slightly stale bread and some rather good wine. Topaz savored it all, thinking that it was probably better than what she'd had to look forward to at the castle. To her surprise, she was finding the company quite preferable, as well.

"So -- I take it that you're a Swynmoor? You can't be a servant girl. You don't talk like one, and your hands are smooth, like a lady's," he said at last.

"Gracious, no!" she exclaimed in reply, "I should probably give you a false name, since you've seen me without any clothes on, but I don't seem to have anything to lose any more."

"What do you mean?" he asked, a bit obtusely.

"Well, I've gone into a strange man's tent naked, so my virtue is permanently compromised, of course. I'm Topaz Stonemont. Lady Topaz Stonemont, so you're right about my not being low born. Lady Swynmoor brought me here because she thought I'd make a good wife for her nephew, but he seems to disagree. Rather strongly, in fact. And after tonight, he'll have a positively fantastic excuse to send me packing. As soon as your army will allow me to leave, that is."

He blinked. How anyone could be offered this radiant girl as a potential bride and turn her down so coldly was simply beyond him. Swynmoor must be off his head, Reynaud thought.

"That's why I was so angry at your army, by the way. It's been rather a disaster since I've arrived, and heaven only knows when I'll be able to go home, since you're laying siege to the castle."

"I hope you understand that any inconvenience I've caused you was entirely --"

"Oh, I know that none of this had anything to do with me. It was just so -- frustrating, so maddening! I suppose I snapped. I'm really the one who should be apologizing, and I certainly do."

He considered several responses, such as "think nothing of it", but all of them seemed absurd, so he remained silent.

"I should probably mention that I've worked out who you are," she added, "You're Reynaud the Black, the man who's leading the ogres and Fomorians. You're quite famous, you know."

"I regret to say that I am, indeed, he."

He bowed slightly from his chair, adding a bit of a flourish with his right hand.

"Surely you're joking? About being sorry, I mean. Half the debutantes in Highreach are in love with you from afar. They swoon over tales of your adventures."

He laughed bitterly, "If only my brothers could hear that! They've always called me a spotty little runt and said that no woman would have me. But I'm sure that if any of those ladies met me in person, their infatuation would end. Promptly. As for my adventures -- they've been highly exaggerated. Most of what I've done since I've left home is try to keep the ogres and Fomorians from killing each other."

"Those two races don't exactly have a history of peace and harmony."

"You see," he said, waving his wine goblet for emphasis, "Even a girl with no military experience understands this -- yet my father hires them both as mercenaries! Not a day goes by when I don't wish that keeping them from each other's throats was his problem! Honestly, he's the one who wants to rule the country, but he sends me out to do the dirty work!"

"I suppose they must be quite angry with me for stepping on their tents," she said quietly.

Reynaud laughed, "You should have seen the looks on their faces! Priceless!"

Topaz suddenly dropped her fork.

"I don't know why I didn't think of this before, but I might have seriously hurt or even killed some of them! I could be a cold-blooded murderer, sitting here, enjoying your food and wine."

"I doubt it," he replied, "When they were demonstrating how tough they were to my father to convince him to hire them, they rolled enormous boulders down mountainsides and allowed themselves to be crushed under them. They emerged from under the rocks, entirely unscathed -- even when they weren't wearing any armor. I can't imagine that a girl's foot would have done them much harm, even an incredibly large one."

"I'm so glad! I'll pay for the damages to your tents, you know."

"Don't worry about it. As far as the Swynmoors are concerned, I'm sure that what you did tonight was just the opening shot in many battles to come. You should have no regrets about fighting the good fight for your side."

"That's just it though -- the Swynmoors don't feel like my side at all. Honestly, I've felt more comfortable with you here tonight than I ever have with my own family."

Reynaud sighed. He'd been thinking something similar, of course, but he simply couldn't allow himself to say it. He was confused enough about this girl already without leading her on like that.

"I suppose I'd better take you back to the castle soon," he said instead, "I don't want anybody to think that I'm taking advantage of your virtue as some sort of spoil of war. It wouldn't do your reputation any good, though I'm ashamed to say that my father might actually encourage that sort of behavior. It'd make me seem more fearsome, you know."

Topaz sighed, as well.

"Not that I have any virtue left, as far as society is concerned. And I'm not eager to go, but I suppose you're right. I've little enough reputation left myself, but I wouldn't want anybody to get the wrong idea about you."

"I suppose we need to figure out how to get you back with a minimum of fuss, then."

They both sipped the last of their wine and pondered, not knowing how to go about it. In the end, Reynaud waited a few more hours, until the Fomorians and ogres were asleep, then he simply rode up to the castle gates. A now-clothed young lady was seated on the back of his horse, though she was still barefoot, since his boots had been hopelessly too big for her. For someone so tall, he thought, her feet were remarkably dainty, like the girl in the story with the fairy godmother and the ball. In any case, Topaz was no longer naked, and she had returned back before sunrise, so the damage to her perceived virtue would be kept as minimal as he could manage.

"Oy, Swynmoor," he called out.

Somewhat to his surprise, the gates were discreetly opened and the drawbridge lowered. Had he been looking for a way to initiate a sneak attack, it would have been perfect. Unfortunately for him in more ways than one, however, Reynaud was an honorable man. His heart sank as she turned and waved at him before the castle gates closed with terrible finality behind her. It was likely that he would never see her again.

4

When the messenger arrived for Lord Tomlin, one of the first places that Waltham went to look for him was the armory. It was sensible enough during a siege, but someone who had served the Moondown family for any length of time could have told you that wasn't really why he was there. Waltham had worked at Swynmoor Castle since he was a boy, just as his father had, before him. If anyone inquired, the old man could have revealed a great number of things about all who lived there, from the lowest scullery maid to Malvern Moondown, the currently absent Earl of Swynmoor himself. No one ever bothered to ask him, though, so the secrets and strange habits of the castle's inhabitants fortunately remained private.

Still, it was rather odd that when Lord Tomlin was troubled about anything, instead of going hunting or drinking his cares away like other young men, he would go to the armory. He'd once mentioned that he liked the feel of all that metal under his hands. There, he'd sharpen his ancestors' swords with a whetstone, polish the centuries-old shields with oil, and clean the rust from suits of armor with sand. The servant was sure that the young lord's preferred means of stress relief meant that his family could boast of one of the best preserved sets of weaponry in all of Highreach. At least, he thought, they might boast if any of them knew that the young man had been doing this for years. They didn't, of course, but Waltham did. When part of your job was locating people in a very large castle if someone was looking for them, it was only sensible to learn something about their habits and preferences. He knocked on the door of the armory and discreetly cleared his throat. It opened, and Lord Tomlin poked his rather tousled head out.

"Yes?" he said, "Oh, it's you, Waltham. What is it? Is Aunt Jilona after me again?"

"No. m'lord. I'm sure you'll be pleased to hear that isn't why I've come."

"Well, that's some good news, at least. There's been entirely too much commotion about the place. Aunts with yapping dogs. Giant girls without any clothes on."

"Yes, m'lord. There certainly has been a great deal of commotion, as you say, and I'm sorry to disturb you when you're in the armory."

"But duty calls and all that. It isn't your fault that it's been like living in the middle of town square here lately. Who's baying for my blood now?"

"A messenger has arrived from Lord Reynaud, saying that he can speak only to you about a matter of some delicacy. Shall I show him in?"

"That's an interesting turn of events. By all means, bring the poor blighter to me straightaway."

"Very good, m'lord."

Shortly, the servant returned with a man dressed in black from head to foot, with a hood that concealed his face. Upon seeing Tom, he reached into his pocket and produced a large silver ring bearing the hedgehog seal of the House of Fynchester. For a moment, the young man wondered whether Reynaud himself had come, but when the messenger revealed his face, it was not him. The man was at least ten years older, and his hair was blonde.

"Lord Swynmoor?"

Tom sighed, "As I've said before, that's my uncle, who's in Finbarr Springs. But I'm the chap you're looking for."

The man nodded, apparently somewhat familiar with the oddness of aristocratic titles.

"My name is Jack, and I'm here to tell you that my lord would have words with you."

"Yes, I presumed that was why he sent you. What's on his mind?"

"Forgive me, m'lord, but I don't know. My message is only that he would speak to you. I don't know what he has to say."

"Ah. So you're here to deliver the message that he has a message for me."

"In a manner of speaking. If you'd be willing, he would meet with you secretly, in the hour before midnight tonight, at The Wounded Soldier. He asks that you come disguised."

"The Wounded Soldier? Has the man no taste in taverns whatsoever? I know he's not from around these parts, but surely The Fox and Geese --"

"Begging your pardon, but he was afraid that you might be recognized there. That's an inn with a good reputation, and you've been known to frequent it in the past. The Wounded Soldier, however --"

"Is practically a house of ill repute. Yes, I'm aware. Not that I've ever actually been there, of course."

"Lord Reynaud guarantees your safety from his men if you'll meet him. Shall I tell him that you'll go?"

"In a place like that, it's not his men I'm worried about. I suppose you'd better let him know I'll join him. Though I don't know how I'll feel about what he has to say if he needs to tell me there. Nonetheless, I'll hear him out like a gentleman."

"Very good, m'lord."

"Here's for your trouble."

He tossed a silver coin to the blonde man, then happily returned to his sharpening and polishing. As Tom worked, he told Waltham what was needed. The servant soon procured an outfit from the clothes chest of one of the absent grooms who worked in the stables. As the young lord looked at himself in the mirror late that night, after the ladies and dogs were asleep, he had to admit that Waltham had chosen well indeed. Not only were there several rips in the clothing, (in places, he was pleased to note, that weren't too embarrassing) it also smelled quite distinctly of horse. If she'd seen him, even his own mother would have had to do a double take to ascertain who he was. Pulling his hood up, he took the secret back passage out of the castle. Even the horse that his servant had waiting for him was old and would raise no comment as the purported steed of a groom on his night off, looking to have a good time in the village.

The Wounded Soldier was located on the same street as the tannery. Mingled with the smells of stale beer and sour wine, the air around the tavern smelled putrid. Tom wasn't sure how anybody could eat in a place like this without throwing up. Still, it was something of an adventure to come to this part of town, and the fact that his aunt would be horrified if she found out was a definite point in its favor. He tied his horse to the hitching post with several others, all of which looked a bit the worse for wear, and went inside. Even for a place that was trying to keep its lamp oil costs low, the tavern was dimly lit, possibly to accommodate the preferences of its patrons. He'd had some fear that he might be recognized, despite his disguise, but as soon as Tom walked through the door, he realized that he needn't have worried. Only a couple of rough-looking men looked up from their drinks when he entered, and they'd quickly turned their eyes back to their wooden mugs. This was plainly a tavern in which you were supposed to mind your own business.

Just as he was wondering whether Fynchester had arrived yet and how he would know if he had, he felt a sharp poke in his left shoulder blade. Although he'd only seen him once before, Tom recognized that the man who had gotten his attention had the face, as well as the dark hair and neatly trimmed beard, of Reynaud the Black. On this night, however, his clothing, which was slightly too large for him, was made up of the showy red and gold hues of a traveling bard. He was even carrying a small harp to complete the outfit. If Tom hadn't been looking for him, he never would have guessed who the man before him was, simply because everyone knew that he dressed exclusively in black.

"Fy --" he began.

"Don't say it," the other man cautioned, "Let's get a booth in a corner, where we can talk."

He nodded, and the two of them claimed the most secluded table they could. A barmaid with several missing teeth came over to take their drink orders, and Reynaud asked for some ale for both of them. Waving away Tom's purse, he paid her in coppers, since a larger denomination might have aroused comment or even suspicion.

"So what's all this cloak and dagger business about, Fynchester?" Tom asked, "If I had any doubts about your honor, I'd suspect that you were trying to bump me off."

"Don't use my title here, you fool. Family names only -- nobody knows them. Mine is Evensea."

"I'm Moondown. Evensea, eh? So that's what you were called at school."

"Only by the teachers. The other boys usually had some dreadful nickname for me, often supplied to them by my own brothers, the louts."

"I always wished I'd had some brothers, myself. It might have been jolly to have someone to play with."

"More trouble than they're worth, I assure you. Or at least mine are."

The barmaid returned with two wooden flagons of ale, flashing her unsettling grin with the dark gaps. He barely managed to suppress a shudder as Reynaud muttered his thanks.

"In any case, I didn't come to talk to you about them."

"No, I didn't suppose you had. Thanks for the first round, by the way."

Just as the darker man started to sputter out a warning, Tom raised the cup to his lips. Mid-swallow, he realized that he had made a terrible mistake, and his eyes bulged out as the first of the brackish brew entered his throat. He banged the mug down on the table with considerable force and glared at Reynaud, who shrugged. At last, he resigned himself to his fate and swallowed the rest of what was in his mouth. Afterwards, gasping for air, he continued to stare accusingly.

"I was going to tell you not to drink that," the dark haired man said mildly.

"You bloody well could have told me sooner," Tom groaned, "You don't need your sword to do me in, apparently. You can poison me and be done with it."

"I'll make it up to you later."

"How? By cutting my tongue out so I'll never taste anything that horrid again?"

Reynaud sighed. This was already not going the way that he'd anticipated. Squaring his jaw, he resolved to get things on the proper footing.

"Look -- Swy -- I mean, Moondown, I really asked you here because I've got something I need to talk to you about, man to man."

"Well, I think that drink put hair on my chest, so you're off to a good start."

"I want -- well, I need, really -- to talk to you about Topaz."

"Topaz? Lady Topaz Stonemont?"

"Yes," he answered, a bit awkwardly, "Look, old chap, I know that she was brought here as a potential wife for you."

"Unfortunately."

"And I wanted to clear it with you before I did anything."

"Did anything?"

"Well," he said, blushing nearly as red as his shirt, "Nothing untoward, you know. Started courting her."

Both men were silent for a moment as the proverbial penny dropped.

"Courting her?" Tom said at last, "Topaz Stonemont?"

"Er, yes."

"You're sweet on Lady Topaz?" he went on, "Gigantic young girl, prone to running about the countryside without a stitch on?"

"I say, there's no need to --"

"Enjoys smashing tents for fun?"

"Really, that was something of a misunderstanding."

"Good Lord, Evensea, if you want to take the girl off my hands, I couldn't be more pleased. I'll buy you whatever you like for a wedding present, as well as christening gifts for each of your undoubtedly enormous children."

"That's getting a bit ahead of things."

"Oh, I don't think so. From what my mother was telling me, she's positively desperate to marry. She'd have you if you were blind, deaf, and afflicted with a limp. Truly, the idea of her having some other poor fool to loom over for the rest of her life gives me nothing but joy."

"Well, I didn't think you'd mind, but I wanted to do the decent thing."

"I'd buy you a drink to wish you happiness, but that seems particularly ill advised," he said, eyeing his flagon with distaste, "Later, when we're somewhere that serves something other than swill."

"There's also that bit of bother with us supposedly being bitter enemies. Are you sure you don't object, on that principle alone?"

"Oh, that. Anybody who offers to free me from the clutches of Lady Topaz Stonemont is like a brother, as far as I'm concerned."

"My brothers are dreadful."

"Right. Forget I said that. Like a cousin, perhaps."

"Better."

"So, what's your next move? Declaring your intentions, I'd suppose."

"About that. The other thing that I wanted to bring up with you, well --"

"Go on, say it, man."

"There's the matter of how difficult it's going to be for me to see her again. I'm sure you understand that I can't exactly court the girl if she's locked away in your castle."

"Yes, I can see the trouble."

"I don't know whether it's quite as big a holiday up North as it is where I come from, but St. Cuthbert's Day is next week --"

"Always a marvelous time! Gallons of beer and wine flowing, loads of people in masks, dancing until dawn. I usually spend it in some sort of costume at The Fox and Geese, but of course, I won't be able to make it out this year. Siege and all."

"That's just the thing, though. Costumes and masks. I was thinking that perhaps you could get some nice girl to accompany you, then the two of you could sneak out -- in disguise, you know -- with Lady Topaz, as well. Then we could all meet up at The Fox and Geese."

"That's a brilliant idea! There's a problem, though. Well, other than the fact that no one could mistake that enormous girl for anyone else."

"Come now, Moondown. You know what bad form it is for anybody to say that they recognize someone on St. Cuthbert's Day. Even if someone notices her, it won't really matter, since they won't be able to tell anyone. What's the other difficulty?"

"I don't have a young lady to go with. Confirmed bachelor, you see."

"Oh, come now, surely there must be somebody! Poor Topaz has had enough challenges to her honor lately, what with her growing out of her dress, then ending up in my tent. There simply must be another lady present!"

"I say, Evensea, that does sound scandalous!"

"But nothing untoward happened, I swear!"

"Well, there is one girl I'd like to ask," Tom said, scratching his chin reflectively.

"That's perfect, then!"

"But I'm not at all sure that she'd agree to join us."

"Why on earth not? Have you said something awful to her?"

"Nothing like that! It's just -- well, she's from the local abbey. Came to deliver the annual taxes and got caught in the castle by the siege."

"A nun? Steady on, old man!"

"No, she's not a nun -- at least, not yet. She's one of the Foundlings. Left on the steps of the abbey as a baby for the sisters to take care of. She's quite the loveliest girl I've ever laid eyes on."

"You positively must ask her, then! If she's with a girl from the abbey, people will definitely not think anything against poor Lady Topaz."

"Well, I'll do my best."

"Excellent! You must send me a message after she accepts! After all, what young woman could refuse an outing with the heir to an earl on St. Cuthbert's Day?"

Tom stood outside the library door, coming perilously close to actually wringing his hands with nervousness. He'd asked Waltham where Kerris might be, and of course, he'd known. Somehow, the old man seemed to always be aware of where everyone in the castle was. It was almost uncanny. If Tom hadn't known him almost literally since he'd first drawn breath, he might have suspected Waltham of witchcraft. It would have been a type of dark arts that had strangely practical applications for a servant. Mildly cursing himself for thinking of the possible magic powers of the staff, rather than working up his courage, he hesitantly knocked on the library door.

"Come in," called a girl's voice from inside.

She was working at the larger of the two tables in the room, with many books spread open before her. As she hunched over a piece of paper, writing with a quill pen, her long golden hair tumbled down next to her flawless face to brush charmingly against the page. This was absolutely dreadful, he thought. What if she refused him? Or worse yet, laughed at him?

"Oh, it's you, my lord," she said, looking up from her work.

Unfortunately, she was still addressing him by his title, but the words no longer dripped with sarcasm, as they had when the two of them been trapped in the closet together.

"Yes, just me, I'm afraid. I'm sorry to bother you when you're studying."

"That's all right," she said, "Did you want to speak to me about something, or are you just looking for somewhere to hide from your aunt again?"

"Oh, Aunt Jilona's off somewhere. Busy trying to find more ridiculous things to put in her hair or hand-feeding her hundreds of horrible little dogs."

Much to his relief, she smiled.

"Ah, so you did actually seek out my company for some reason, my lord."

"Yes. Though I do wish you'd call me Tom -- especially given what I'm about to say."

She grinned even more broadly.

"This does sound like it may have been worth taking a moment or two from my work, then."

"It's just -- you do celebrate St. Cuthbert's Day in the abbey?"

"There's a special mass in honor of him, yes. And at supper, we have a cup or even two of the first of the ale or wine that's ready for the year. It's a treat for us, and we look forward to it each year, especially the Foundling girls."

"Perhaps you know that it can be a bit more -- merry of a holiday when one doesn't live in an abbey."

She nodded.

"Our priest preached a sermon against it last year. All of that drinking led quite a few of the village men to fight. And the disguises made women more willing to do forbidden things, since their reputations weren't so much at risk."

"It can get a bit wild, I suppose."

"Father Jerome said it was fortunate that we almost never leave the abbey. Our isolation preserves us from sin."

"About that. I was wondering if you'd be willing to do a girl a favor in that regard."

"What do you mean?"

"You remember Topaz Stonemont, the young lady that Aunt Jilona wants me to marry?"

"Everyone in the castle has been talking about how she was running around outside, naked as a newborn baby. I would think that your aunt would have found her actions scandalous and started looking for a new bride for you."

"Well, let's just say that whole business was a bit of a misunderstanding."

"How could anyone mistake the intentions of a girl who threw off her dress and ran outside? If she's not sinful, the only other explanation is that she must be raving mad."

"Wait -- all you've heard is that she tossed off her clothes at supper and began gallivanting around in the altogether?"

"Yes. How could there possibly be any more to a story like that?"

"Well, there was a -- magical mishap. For some reason no one can fathom, she started growing uncontrollably at the supper table. She became so enormous that her gown ripped off of her."

Kerris dropped her pen, an astonished look on her face.

"So that was what happened. I don't really know the young lady, but she hardly seemed like the sort who would -- well, the poor girl! And you saw the whole thing?"

"Heavens, no! Not everything! Not anything, really. She made it out of the room before it became apparent that her dress wasn't going to last much longer."

"And you'd like me to help her regain her reputation?"

"In a manner of speaking. You see, even after all that, there seems to be a chap who's keen to marry her."

"How fortunate for her that you're willing to overlook what happened."

"Oh, no. Not me -- I don't fancy of lifetime of looking my wife square in the neck. Another man entirely. But he can't get to know her under the present circumstances. And that's where you come in."

"But what could I possibly do?"

"Well, being from the abbey, you've got quite an air of respectability. I was hoping that you could accompany the two of them on an outing."

"As a chaperone, you mean?"

"Well, something like that. But there's a bit more to it..."

Against her better judgment, nearly a week later, Kerris found herself in a gown and mask that were meant to make her look like a stylized orange and white cat. One of Lady Swynmoor's St. Cuthbert's Day costumes from ages ago, it was the most elaborate outfit that the Foundling girl had worn in her entire life. There was a half-mask, encrusted with tiny beads and winking jewels, that left her mouth exposed, and the dress itself was covered in ribbons and lace. It even had a white velvet tail at the back, the tip of which was adorned with an enormous golden bow. She smelled like moth balls and felt absolutely ridiculous. Topaz, of course, was far too tall to be able to wear a gown that had belonged to either of the Swynmoor ladies. However, Waltham had been able to find a faerie mask on a beribboned stick and some gossamer wings for her to borrow, which Lady Glynis had worn for a previous year's festivities. They shimmered and winked ostentatiously as she bounced on the high heels of her satin shoes with excitement, the perfect accessories for her bright green dress.

The young ladies were hiding from prying eyes in the stairwell that Topaz had used during her unfortunate growing incident. Today, she had claimed another headache, telling the older ladies that she would be taking her meals in her room until she felt better. As they waited, Tom was making his own excuses for why he wouldn't be available that afternoon, explaining to his mother and aunt that he had confidential business related to the siege. Since she'd been excused from servants' duties, no one seemed to care much where Kerris was spending her time, so she hadn't needed to make anything up at all.

"Isn't this exciting?" asked Topaz, somewhat rhetorically.

"I can't believe I let him talk me into this. What would Sister Goldrose say?"

"This must be your first St. Cuthbert's Day away from the abbey.

How amusing for you!"

Just as the smaller girl was about to respond, Tom came striding down the stairs, dressed as a pirate, complete with his own bejeweled half-mask, cutlass, and a large captain's hat, as well as the bird that his aunt had worn in her hair. It now sat on his shoulder, looking as startled as ever.

"Yarr, ladies," he said, bowing elaborately, "Be ye ready for a merry time?"

The tall girl nodded enthusiastically. Nervously, Kerris bit her bottom lip.

The Fox and Geese was as different from The Wounded Soldier as night was from day. There was a spacious stable available for their horses, instead of just a hitching post. As they approached the door, rhythmic sounds of pipes and drums could be heard through the open windows. There were also the delicious smells of several kinds of meat pies wafting out, as well as the scents of fresh beer and sweet wine. As soon as Tom had opened the door for the ladies, the Foundling girl could see many costumed couples twirling about in a country dance. Many of the masked patrons who were had remained seated were clapping along with the music or keeping time by pounding their mugs on the carved wooden tables.

"How will we find out which one is Reynaud?" Topaz asked.

"He knows what our costumes are, and he told me that he'll be dressed as a green dragon. And I'm sorry to mention it, but even in disguise, my lady, you're fairly unmistakable."

"Perhaps this once my height will serve me well. I'll be able to see him in the crowd better, too," she said.

Looking around the room, she soon caught sight of a dark-haired man in a green dragon costume sitting on a barstool, a pewter mug in his hand.

"That must be him!" Topaz announced.

She wasted no time in getting over to the bar, practically pushing customers and servers alike out of her way as she navigated through the revelry. Everyone seemed to be having far too good of a time to mind.

"Good heavens, she's like a bloodhound that's scented a fox. We'd better try to keep up with her, if we're meant to safeguard her reputation," Kerris said.

Nodding, Tom grabbed onto the cat costumed girl's arm and guided her expertly around the dancers and drinkers, who were already decidedly tipsy, despite the fact that it was only noon. By the time they had pushed their way through, the man who had, indeed, turned out to be Reynaud had already begun a shouted conversation with Lady Topaz.

"Yarr -- Happy St. Cuthbert's Day to ye!" Tom yelled over the music.

The dragon rose from his stool and clapped him heartily on the arm.

"Moondown! How splendid to see you! Or at least, I presume that's you! You told me you were going to be a pirate, but really, what a fabulous disguise! I had to content myself with what I could buy in the village, practically at the last moment!"

There was no room for him to turn around, but he held his arms out, displaying the silk scales that had been sewn beneath his arms, which continued all along his sides to end just above his knees. By coincidence, or perhaps fate, his outfit was precisely the same shade of green as Topaz's faerie costume.

"No, no, you look wonderful!"

"And I presume this lovely cat is your young lady from the abbey!"

"Well, I wouldn't say she's mine, but yes, this is Kerris Seaborn."

He chivalrously bent over her hand but decorously refrained from kissing it.

"Pleased to meet you! I'm Reynaud Evensea." he shouted over the chaos.

"Oh, look! A group of people left their booth just now! Quick -- let's claim it before anyone else gets there first!" said Topaz.

With the tall woman leading the way, they managed to get there in time, as a plump barmaid, whom Tom was pleased to note had all of her teeth, was removing the plates and mugs.

"Welcome, friends," she said, "Let me take these to the kitchen, and I'll come back to find out what you'll have."

Almost as soon as she sat down, Topaz began clapping along to the music, watching the dancers through her faerie mask with shining eyes.

"You like dancing?" Reynaud asked.

"Very much," she answered.

"Care to give it a go with me?"

"Really?" she replied, nearly squeaking in her enthusiasm, "You don't mind that I'm taller than you?"

The dark haired man laughed, "Today, it's only a faerie that's taller than a dragon. But no, I wouldn't mind. If any man had something to say about it, I'd give him a good punch in the nose."

Laughing with delight, she took his hand, and the two of them picked their way over to the dance floor. Despite the fact that she was wearing wings that protruded nearly a foot from her back, Topaz immediately began bouncing and twirling as gracefully as a doll in a music box, effortlessly keeping up with all of the steps. She was well matched in Reynaud, who seemed to know his parts of the dance as well as she remembered her own. They were so skillful that several of the other revelers fell back to watch them, clapping and stomping from the sidelines.

"Well, I'll be stewed!" said Tom, bemused.

"They certainly do look good together," Kerris agreed.

"You don't want to join them, do you? I'm apparently no Reynaud, but I've been known --"

She shook her head.

"I'm sorry, but they don't teach us any dance steps at the abbey," she said, a bit regretfully.

Just then, the barmaid returned.

"So, what'll you have?" she asked.

"Go on, get anything you like. I'll pay, of course," said the young man.

The Foundling girl had to admit to herself that, despite the strangeness of her surroundings, she was positively starving. By the time she and Tom were done, they had ordered several meat pies, including the house special -- a venison one -- and a round of drinks for everyone. After that, however, there didn't seem to be much to say, and they sat there for a few moments, looking at each other. Tom tried to dispel the awkwardness.

"So, about the actual Saint Cuthbert --" he began.

Just then, there was a commotion as several men in what seemed to be very elaborate costumes entered the inn. Everyone turned to look as a group of people who, for all the world, looked like ogres and Fomorians came through the door. There was a brief hush, then some of the patrons began to applaud. The hideously costumed men looked surprised, then waved at everyone as they made their way directly to the bar.

"Gracious! They must have been working on their costumes all year!" Topaz said.

She took her partner's dragon-scaled hand for a series of dance steps that began with a spin. Peering over her shoulder to look at the men who had just joined the party, Reynaud realized something crucial that the rest of the revelers did not. Immediately, he felt all joy drain from his frame like the air from a balloon. What on earth were they doing there? He was going to wring his generals' enormous necks when he got back to the encampment tonight.

"Forgive me," he said, "But I absolutely must attend to something."

"Oh, but we were having such fun!" she protested mildly.

He escorted a somewhat disappointed Topaz back to the booth, then made his way over to where several members of his army were ordering large quantities of drinks.

"What in the bloody hell are you doing here?" he demanded.

"Izir say you come here to have party. We want to drink too," said a Fomorian.

"And dance," added one of the ogres.

Reynaud shook his head, trying to erase that image from his mind.

"You absolutely cannot be here! Go back to the camp immediately! The only reason that your presence hasn't caused a riot is that people think you're men in costume."

"But Commander," another Fomorian protested, "We celebrate. You have victory over giant girl."

The rest of the ogres and Fomorians nodded enthusiastically.

"Now she will not come near us again."

"You're really a pack of idiots, aren't you? Do you see that girl over there dressed as a faerie? That's her, sitting with Lord Swynmoor and a girl from the local abbey. They're here with me."

As one creature, all of his enormous mercenaries turned their heads to where Topaz was sitting with Tom and Kerris, helping herself to a slice of meat pie.

"That her? Giant girl? With Swynmoor? You very smart, Commander! This ambush!"

"No, they're my friends, and it is positively not --" he began.

Before the rest of the sentence could leave his mouth, the ogres and Fomorians were on their feet, knocking several barstools over in the process.

"Don't worry, Commander, we'll get them!" an ogre reassured him.

"Oh, dear God!" he shouted, "Topaz! Moondown! Run -- run for your lives!"

But the three young people from Swynmoor castle couldn't hear him over the music and the babble of voices, as well as the pervasive sounds of eating and drinking. Looking up from his pork pie, all Tom saw was that at least half a dozen ogres and Fomorians were coming toward them at full speed, with Reynaud seemingly urging them on from the bar. Apparently, the whole thing had been a trap. He dropped his fork and grabbed each of the girls by the elbow.

"Ladies -- I'm afraid it's time for us to take our leave! Now!"

The musicians abruptly stopped playing as the three of them made a break for the door. Some of the other revelers, realizing the truth about the creatures' lack of costumes, also began to scream and flee. They added to the general confusion, getting in between the mercenaries and their intended captives. However, hampered by her long dress and high heeled shoes, Topaz was the slowest of the companions, and the Fomorians laid hands on her before she could escape. Although Kerris was also wearing a gown, she still had her sensible shoes on from the abbey, so she was able to make it to the stables safely. Tom, dressed more sensibly than either of the girls in boots and breeches, easily got to the entrance of the inn. Eyes narrowing, he turned to look back at the tall girl in the even larger soldiers' clutches, suddenly convinced that she had been complicit in the whole plot. Just before he escaped, he caught Reynaud's eye. The dark man was standing perfectly still in the chaos, his dragon mask fallen from his face.

"How could you?" Tom mouthed clearly.

Before Reynaud could respond, the other young lord had turned on his heel and run after Kerris. The black haired man knew that his friend, as well as any future hope of peace, was gone.

5

Tom and Kerris arrived back at Swynmoor castle exhausted and thirsty. Their garments were torn, and the horses had been ridden into a lather. Somewhere along the way, she had lost a shoe, a rather ironic occurrence, since it had been her sensible footwear that allowed her to escape from Reynaud's mercenaries. The young lord wanted to have a quiet drink with the Foundling girl and find out if she truly was all right, since she hadn't said a word to him since they left The Fox and Geese. Once her well-being had been established, he planned to return to the armory and hold the reassuring solidity of swords and shields in his hands again. At least iron, silver and copper could be depended on not to betray him. As soon as they'd dismounted, however, he saw Waltham approaching, a sheepish look on his face.

"M'lord?" the old servant began.

"Go on. It's all right -- I know what you're going to say."

"Your aunt and your mother are anxious to see you immediately, m'lord."

"I thought as much from your hangdog expression. Where are they?"

"In Lady Swynmoor's sitting room."

"Ah, the dragon's lair itself. I'll join them as soon as I've changed my clothes and had something to drink. I can hardly face my executioners dressed as a pirate."

"Forgive me, m'lord, but her ladyship was very adamant on this point. I am to conduct you to her sitting room the moment you return. No delays are to be allowed for any reason."

Tom sighed. He supposed it couldn't be helped.

"Very well. Don't worry -- it's not your fault that Aunt Jilona is being so unreasonable. Kerris and I will be there directly."

"I must apologize again, but she emphasized that I should bring you alone."

"Honestly," he groaned, then turned to the Foundling girl, "I'm afraid that both duty and my Aunt Jilona call rather urgently. Perhaps we can have lunch together tomorrow and --"

She stared at him silently for a moment, glowering fiercely. Then, she turned on her heel -- the one that still had a shoe on it -- and stalked off, not deigning to reply.

"It seems that all the ladies in the castle have a bone to pick with me. Women, eh, Waltham?"

"Indeed, m'lord. Now, if you'll allow me to conduct you to Lady Swynmoor's sitting room."

He gave an exaggerated salute.

"Those who are about to die salute you."

His aunt was seated in the largest, most ornate chair that was available. Her dress was, by far, the most headache-inducing one she'd produced yet, with screamingly bright scarlet whorls competing for attention with enormous orange dots. The overall effect was positively nauseating, and he was relieved that there hadn't been time to drink more at the inn. Even sober, looking at her brought on an almost overwhelming urge to sink down onto the floor from vertigo. Dogs were clustered around her voluminous skirts, and the moment he entered the room, all of them began yapping shrilly. His mother was sitting to the left of Aunt Jilona in a considerably less elaborate chair, her lips pursed with worry. The fingers of his aunt's right hand were drumming steadily on a small ornamental table. She looked like a grim queen about to give the command for his head to be cut off. Somberly, he took off the enormous pirate captain's headgear, then untied the mask and placed it inside of the hollow part of the hat. He stood there, holding it awkwardly. Wrinkling her nose in distaste, his aunt stood and took a few steps over to him. Indignantly, she plucked her now disheveled bird from his shoulder. She sat down again, trying hopelessly to smooth its feathers.

"Well, Tomlin, what can you possibly have to say for yourself?" she demanded.

What he absolutely could not do, he decided, was panic. He wasn't even sure how much she knew. If he wasn't careful, he would divulge more information than was strictly necessary, getting him even deeper into trouble.

"Well, as you can probably deduce from my costume, I slipped into town to celebrate St. Cuthbert's Day. It probably wasn't the most prudent decision, but youthful high spirits --"

"Youthful high spirits! Is this the excuse I'll offer to Lady Stonemont, when I have to explain why her daughter has been kidnapped?"

"Really, Tom, what could you have been thinking of? You might have been killed!" his mother added.

"Perhaps that would have been best for the Moondown family line! As it is, future generations will be infected with his foolishness! If only Malvern were here, he could deal with you properly!"

Several of the little dogs punctuated this statement with an emphatic bark or two.

"Hang on a moment -- how do you know that Topaz is missing? She's meant to be in her room with a headache."

"Meant to be, yes. Tragically, however, she is not. My maid convinced me that there was no harm in allowing her to go to The Fox and Geese with our game keeper to celebrate St. Cuthbert's day. She soon recognized Lady Topaz, of course, because of her height --"

"So much for the idea that no one would admit to knowing who she was," he muttered.

"But she was positively shocked to discover that the young lady had apparently left the castle with you. That pirate costume isn't much of a disguise, you know. Anyhow, my poor maid simply couldn't decide what to do, especially when Lady Topaz started dancing with another young man entirely! Just as she'd made up her mind to insist that both of you accompany her back to the castle at once, you were attacked!"

His mother broke in, "By ogres and Fomorians -- mercenaries of Reynaud the Black! Poor Topaz! Heaven knows what indignities she'll suffer --"

"Really, Glynis, you must refrain from speaking about that. It's bad enough that the girl has completely lost her reputation without giving in to idle speculation and gossip."

His mother looked chagrined.

"Now, see here, Aunt Jilona --"

"Really, Tomlin, under the circumstances, I'm not sure how you dare to say 'see here'!"

"If she's suffering any indignities, they're her own fault!" he burst out.

"What a terrible thing to say," his mother said.

"Tomlin Moondown -- not another word from you! When your uncle returns, I'll see that he has you horsewhipped!"

"I'm dreadfully sorry, Aunt Jilona, but I really must insist that you listen! Lady Topaz conspired with Reynaud to set those mercenaries on Kerris and me! It was all a trap, and she helped to spring it!"

There was a pause as his aunt deliberately put the ruined bird down on the gilded table that was at her elbow. She detached an absurdly ornate fan that had been hooked onto her bodice, snapped it open and fluttered it rapidly, setting her mouth in a dangerous line. A dog chose that inopportune moment to yap, and she lightly tapped it with the fan to shush it.

"You have one chance to explain what you mean by those remarks," she said, ominously.

"And tell us who on earth this Kerris girl is," added his mother.

"That will do, Glynis," his aunt said icily, glaring at his mother if she'd like to hit her with the fan, as well.

Giving up on his original plan of obfuscation, he explained it all. The late-night meeting with Reynaud at The Wounded Soldier. Asking Kerris to accompany him to the festivities. Topaz's surprising facility with country dance steps. Reynaud's betrayal. At last, he looked up at the older ladies, his hands spread, unsure of what they would make of it.

"Well," his aunt said at last, "That's quite a story,"

"It's true!" he insisted.

"I never said that I doubted the truth of your explanation, as dubious as it might seem to anybody who hadn't known you since birth. The fact that you would set foot in The Wounded Soldier says as much about your shameful lack of judgment as the fact that, against all common sense, you trusted Reynaud the Black! It's that man's sworn duty to deprive you of your home, your lands -- everything that your family has worked to build for generations! And you nearly threw it all away because you didn't like the girl I'd chosen for you!"

"If you're fond of this young lady from the abbey, you should bring her to tea," his mother interjected.

"Glynis, I must positively demand that you desist! This is hardly the time or the place --"

"But if he's interested in somebody --"

"At the moment, she doesn't seem to be speaking to me," he said.

"I'm sure she'll come around if you just apologize."

"No, she's really furious."

"Honestly -- have the both of you gone positively barking mad?" his aunt interrupted, shrilly.

Her tone set off a chorus of yapping from the dogs. Many of them also stood on their hind legs or began running in circles excitedly. The cacophony was tremendous enough that the three of them had to wait until the chaos subsided somewhat before anybody could continue. Aunt Jilona shut her fan and bent down to pet as many of them as she could soothingly without getting up from her chair.

"Hush, Fifi! Lulu, please!" she could be heard saying when the noise died down slightly.

At last, the barking quieted, and his aunt resumed her habitual rigid posture. Although gentlemen weren't supposed to have such thoughts, Tom had often wondered if she sat that way because of the stiffness of her bodices.

"As you requested, I've listened to your explanation. Now it's your turn to listen to me. When I brought that girl here, I assured her mother -- my good friend -- that she would be under my protection. Since she's been at Swynmoor Castle, she's grown to gigantic proportions for no reason anyone can fathom, run outside stark naked, and gotten herself captured by Reynaud the Black! My purpose in bringing Lady Topaz here was to arrange a good marriage for her, not to ensure that she'd become ineligible for any match whatsoever!"

"But -- but she's going to marry Reynaud!" he sputtered.

"Honestly, Tomlin, there seems to be no end to your gullibility. That man has lied about everything. And do you know that only last week, he and his despicable army raided the village of Swynmoor to steal pots and pans? The horrible brute didn't even spare the cookware of orphans or old ladies! Why on earth would you think that he's sincere in his supposed affections for Lady Topaz? He was using the poor misguided girl to get to you."

"Steady on, Aunt Jilona! He's done a pretty low thing today, but --" he began.

"Steady on yourself, you hare-brained boy. Now, I am about to tell you what is going to happen. You will rescue that girl from Reynaud the Black's clutches and bring her back to Swynmoor Castle!"

"I haven't got any soldiers! How on earth --"

"I don't know, and I don't care. You're the one who studied military strategy and history for years at a very expensive school. Use that education for once, and work it out!"

"But I --"

"And once she's safe and sound, you will marry Lady Topaz. Promptly. I will simply not permit the damage to her family's reputation -- which you have caused -- to remain!"

"Aunt Jilona, be reasonable!"

"You are dismissed!"

"But --"

"Dis-missed!" she said firmly, pronouncing each syllable.

She decisively snapped her fan open again and glared down her nose at him. There was nothing for Tom to do but leave the room.

Once Aunt Jilona was through with him, he didn't have the heart to seek Kerris out, since he would only hear what would undoubtedly be more harsh words. He was about to head directly to the armory when his stomach grumbled audibly. He'd had no time to take more than a forkful or two of his pork pie before the ogres and Fomorians had descended, and he was absolutely ravenous. Tom decided to stop off in the larder before proceeding to spend the rest of the day sharpening swords and cleaning suits of armor. Tucking the pirate hat under his arm, he headed downstairs instead of up.

When he reached the kitchen, he was struck by how empty it was. Ordinarily, it would have been full of servants that, startled by his presence, would have immediately snapped to attention and asked politely what he wanted. But nearly all of them were gone, unable to return to the castle during the siege. Stupid Reynaud, he thought, perhaps he really was enough of a scoundrel to steal old women's pots and pans. As it was, only the cook was there, and she was taking her habitual afternoon nap in the chair beside the fire. She had to rise very early each morning to start breakfast for everybody, and there was usually a lull in her activities between lunch and dinner. She often took advantage of the time by catching a bit of sleep. Moving quietly so as not to wake her, Tom slipped past her into the larder.

Considerably smaller than the kitchen, this room was cool and filled with inviting smells. Taking a cloth napkin that had inexplicably been left on one of the shelves, he peered around in the dimly lit space to see what might be available for a late lunch. Unsheathing the pirate cutlass, he lopped off a bit of bread from a half-loaf that seemed to be beckoning to him, then added a bit of white cheese to accompany it.

"Yarrr, plunder," he muttered under his breath.

There was also an end of cured sausage that was sitting there, looking inviting. Presumably, it had been among the provisions that his aunt had brought from Finbarr Springs. Well, her little dogs wouldn't be getting that one. He speared it decisively on the end of his knife. Only one thing could make this generously sized snack complete, he thought. He found the barrels of pickles that had been brought from the abbey and removed a stopper from the top of one of them, hoping that it wasn't sauerkraut. To his satisfaction, he discovered that it was red peppers. He took several and laid them on top of his improvised sandwich, then carefully replaced the large cork, so the rest wouldn't spoil.

After pausing at the ale kegs to fill a silver mug for himself, he brought his improvised meal up to the armory. There, he gratefully settled onto the stool he'd transported there years ago and took the first few bites of his food. The sausage tasted pleasingly of fennel, and the spicy pickles complemented it perfectly. He picked a red pepper off of the meat and popped it into his mouth, crunching reflectively. At the moment, he wasn't particularly pleased with men, women, or even dogs. Perhaps he could retreat to a mountaintop somewhere and become a holy hermit. He could always bring a few cats into the arrangement, since they, at least, had done nothing against him. He sighed, determined to get to work. He was so tired after his ordeal that he could scarcely bear the thought of getting up to find a blade that needed sharpening.

Tom stretched out an arm in the general direction of the swords, wishing that he could summon one of them to come to him. Much to his astonishment, several of them rose into the air. Blinking, he dropped his hand back to his side, and they clattered down into the pile from which they had arisen. He shook his head. Apparently, the stress was truly getting to him. He took a long swig of ale and finished off the last few bites of his food, feeling the reassuring tingle of hot peppers against his tongue. He experimentally stretched his arm out again, this time in the general direction of the shields that had been set aside for polishing. As if in a dream, the top two floated up into the air and hovered there mysteriously. He recoiled, letting his hand fall again, and they crashed to the ground.

Deciding to try an experiment, he waved his hand over the remains of his lunch. While the napkin obeyed the laws of gravity and remained on the floor, the silver flagon flew up about two feet and stayed there. He moved his arm to the left, and the cup floated in the same direction beneath his hand. As he brought his arm up, the mug rose accordingly. When his hand returned to his side, the silver mug fell noisily to the ground. He laughed out loud. Magic seemed to abound in Swynmoor Castle lately, causing everything from suddenly gigantic girls to the unexpected ability to control metal. He simply had to show someone what he could do.

Running through a mental list of people that he could possibly demonstrate the newfound ability to, he realized that there basically wasn't anyone who wasn't furious at him or hadn't recently betrayed him. Waltham would watch his display of magic, but showing him would inevitably be anticlimactic. The old man would simply nod unflappably and say "impressive, m'lord", before returning to his duties. His mother hadn't seemed angry, but she would probably worry about utterly absurd and unlikely ways in which he could hurt himself (and others) with the new power. Well, that was disappointing, he thought. Idly, he waved a few fingers, causing several daggers that were near his feet to do a little dance in the air. If showing somebody wasn't an option, what could he do? Suddenly, he sat bolt upright, struck with inspiration. This, he believed, could solve everything. He hurried back to his room to change out of the ridiculous pirate costume. He needed to find something brown and green to wear if this plan was going to succeed.

Eschewing a horse, Tom slipped outside and began the descent on foot. He did not enter the tent city that stood at the foot of the hill, instead sneaking around its perimeter to the edges of the forest. It was certainly to his advantage that he had lived here since he was born; he knew the area like the back of his hand. He easily located the tree that he'd been thinking of. It was extremely tall, thick, and sturdy. He had often climbed it as a boy and knew it would easily hold his weight. Better still, its limbs were so long that quite a few of them stretched out directly over the encampment. He silently cursed himself for not testing how close he had to be to a metal object to make it obey his wishes. All he could do now was hope that it would work from the distance he had in mind. Placing his foot on the lowest branch, he began to climb. After a somewhat dizzying ascent, he found a thick branch that enabled him to shinny directly over top of the camp. He looked down, silently thanking God that he had no fear of heights. As he'd hoped, he could see everything, though even the Fomorians looked like dolls from this distance.

Back in his tent and wearing black again, Reynaud read the letter a second time, frowning. Despite his initial irrational fears, it was, of course, too soon for his father to have heard about today's debacle. The news that he'd had the heir to the house of Swynmoor within easy reach of him, but hadn't killed him, would probably make his father apoplectic. He certainly wasn't looking forward to the next message from home. As it was, the current missive from his father chastised him for wasting valuable time and energy on last week's village raid. He grumbled, actually shaking his fist at the paper in frustration. Despite what his father thought, it had been truly necessary to obtain replacements for the cooking supplies that the ogres had tossed into the river. His entire ancestral homeland, his father claimed, was laughing at him and his army. There was even a humorous song circulating throughout the court about his recent foray into town, called the "Cookie Baking Raid of Reynaud the Black Aproned".

The dark haired man tossed the letter into the fire. He had more important things on his mind than his family's perpetual disappointment with him. Just when Reynaud had thought that he and Moondown were becoming friends, the other young lord started to believe that he'd betrayed and ambushed him. For the life of him, he couldn't figure out how to correct the misunderstanding, since he was sure that Swynmoor wouldn't agree to another meeting. Even worse, he had Lady Topaz in his camp again, with no appropriate means of sending her back to the castle with her reputation intact a second time. Of course, there was no denying that it was extremely pleasant to have her company. But he didn't want to obtain it like this, in a way that practically guaranteed that she would be shunned by polite society for the rest of her life. He sighed. She was the only girl Reynaud ever thought he would actually want to marry someday, but only slightly more than a week after he'd met her, he was ruining her life.

Suddenly, he heard yet another commotion outside. There was the unsettling sound of metal clanking against metal, and some of his mercenaries seemed to be howling in pain. Steadying himself for whatever he might see, the dark young man stepped outside of his tent. Purloined cooking pots were flying through the air, banging loudly into each other repeatedly to make a terrible noise. As he watched, a frying pan hurtled up from where it had been lying on the ground to smack one of the ogres soundly across the face, causing him to scream in pain. Reynaud squeezed his eyelids tightly shut, hoping that the whole ridiculous business would stop as easily as it seemed to have started. He opened them again, but there was no such luck. A stew pot was careening toward his face, end over end, threatening to bash his skull in. Instinctively, he ducked, and it flew over his head to thud solidly in the mud behind him. As he watched in horror, two saucepans lifted themselves from the ground and positioned themselves on either side of an oblivious Fomorian's large, warty head.

"Look out!" he shouted.

He dove into the enormous mercenary, knocking him down just before the two pans clanged together where his head had been, moments before. The huge creature looked at him.

"You save me, Commander," he said.

"Never mind that. What in blazes is going on?"

"The cooking things we take from the village --"

"Yes?"

"They cursed -- because we steal them! They fly around by themself, hitting us to punish us! Give them back, Commander, and say we sorry."

"I don't think that's why our cookware has suddenly decided to --"

As if a second sense had triggered it, he suddenly felt the overwhelming urge to look up mid-sentence. He saw a groggy Lady Topaz pushing her tent flaps aside and yawning, as if she had just woken up from a nap. A bread knife was hurtling toward her, threatening to impale her with its blade. He sprung up from where he was lying on the ground and ran toward her, drawing his sword as he moved. He barely had enough time to notice the look of surprise registering on her face before he reached her side, imposing his body between her and the deadly blade. Extending his sword, he nimbly knocked the bread knife off its course, deflecting it with a clatter. It bounced off of his sword and embedded itself in the ground, twanging with the force of the blow.

"Reynaud --" she began, eyes widening.

"Never mind. Get back into your tent and stay as low to the ground as possible, understand?" he tersely instructed her.

Nodding silently, she retreated. He was pleased that she wasn't one of those females who would freeze up in times of danger. Crouching down, sword still drawn, Reynaud scanned the camp, alert for the next move of the apparently rebellious cookware.

Up in the tree, Tom was grinning from ear to ear, enjoying himself immensely. It was the most fun he'd had since Aunt Jilona arrived. And it was no more than the treacherous Fynchester and his wretched mercenary army deserved, he thought. His mouth fell open in horror, however, as Topaz stepped out of her tent just as he sent a knife flying through the air. He tried to shout a warning to her, but the girl couldn't hear him over the sounds of iron and copper cookware smashing into things, as well as the shouts of ogres and Fomorians. His whole body sagged with relief as he watched Reynaud bravely throwing himself into the fray to save her. Although she'd been working against the house of Swynmoor, brutally stabbing a young girl with a bread knife had not been part of his plan.

Unfortunately, he found that momentarily relaxing was not a good idea when one was sitting on a tree limb. Losing balance, he fell, narrowly saving himself by catching onto the branch with both hands. Lower down, all of the pots and pans that had been careening about abruptly fell to the ground. He began struggling desperately to pull himself up, as the tree branch began to shake alarmingly with his weight. Tom swore, realizing what a fool he'd been not to take into account that he'd gained quite a few pounds since he'd last climbed this tree at the age of eleven. Trying to jar the tree limb as little as possible, he managed to swing himself up enough to heave his right knee over the branch. He had just enough time to smile at his success before the cracking sounds started.

"No, don't!" he implored.

Apparently impervious to his pleading, the wood split and broke with a sound that seemed to Tom like a cannon firing. Still holding onto the branch, he dropped through the air, hitting another tree limb on the way down.

"Ugh!" he cried out.

He shouted in pain and terror each time he hit another branch as he fell. Fortunately for him, there were many, and they served to break his fall. Even more luckily, he ultimately crashed onto a brightly colored tent, which collapsed almost gracefully with the impact, like a woman spreading her skirts wide for a curtsey. With surprising slowness, he continued his fall, finishing at last on his back atop a pile of striped fabric. It was only then that his hands relaxed enough for him to let go of the tree limb he'd been grasping the entire way down. Tom lay on the ground, eyes tightly closed, trying to catch his breath and mentally assess the damage. He moved his arms, then his legs, followed by his head. He concluded that he'd had the wind knocked out of him, and there was scarcely a part of his body that didn't have a rapidly darkening bruise, but he wasn't seriously hurt. He opened his eyes.

Immediately, he wished he hadn't. Standing over him, sword drawn threateningly, was Reynaud the Black. Somewhat painfully, the lighter haired young man flung his arms above his head, hoping to disarm his adversary by sending the weapon hurtling through the air. Obligingly, the sword leapt out of Fynchester's hand, but instead of being cast far away, it simply embedded itself in the earth next to him with a soft thunk. The mysterious force that allowed him to have power over metal seemed to be getting weaker. He scrambled awkwardly to his feet and motioned with both arms toward himself, trying to bring the weapon to him. It quivered and fell over on its side. Reynaud simply watched all of his efforts calmly with a hand on one hip and a bemused look on his face.

"So, you can control metal," he said at last, "That could be very useful indeed."

The lighter haired young man gave up, dropping both arms to his sides, defeated.

"Well, I can't usually," he admitted, "For some reason -- today, I can."

"How on earth did that happen?"

"Why did Lady Topaz grow to at least ten times her size?"

"Touché."

"I suppose you're going to hold me hostage, so that my family will give up," Tom said, resignedly.

"That is the idea, yes. Though I admit to having a certain desire to turn you over to my army, since you attempted to impale poor Lady Topaz with a bread knife."

There was a general rumble of assent and encouragement for this plan from the mercenaries.

"That was an accident!" Tom protested, "She came out at precisely the wrong moment! On my honor as a gentleman, I was so relieved you saved her that I lost my balance and fell out of the tree."

With a rustle, a nearby tent's flaps parted, and the tall girl emerged a second time. The lighter haired young lord was now close enough to notice that she was dressed in Fynchester's black clothes again.

"I seem to be hearing my name being bandied about quite a bit. Reynaud, I presume it's safe to come out now?"

"Yes. It was this scoundrel here who was causing all the trouble."

"Scoundrel! You're the bounder who lured me to The Fox and Geese to ambush me! After I risked getting into trouble with my Aunt Jilona so you could dance with the girl you wanted to marry!"

"He said that he wanted to marry me?" Topaz interjected, blushing.

"I did no such thing! Ambushing Swynmoor, that is!" he quickly added as her expression darkened, "I suppose I did tell him that I was thinking -- well -- in that way about you."

"Oh, Reynaud," she said, smiling and looking down at her feet.

Tom whirled to face the girl a bit unsteadily, still shaken from his fall.

"And you! You conspired with him to do it! After my family's extended every hospitality! Why it's -- downright ungrateful!"

"How dare you impugn Lady Topaz's honor! She did nothing of the kind! I was telling these lunkheads," the dark man said, waving broadly at the mercenaries, "To leave the inn at once, when they attacked you against my orders! She's never so much as said a word against your family."

"So the two of you hadn't planned an ambush all along?"

"No!" Topaz and Reynaud both shouted emphatically at the same time.

"Ah. Well, I suppose that changes things, then," Tom said, a bit sheepishly, "I suppose you didn't steal cookware from the villagers either, as my Aunt Jilona said?"

"Well, I did do that, I'm afraid," he admitted, "But nobody was harmed. And it was only because the ogres threw the pots and pans we'd brought into a river."

"Serves you right, then," the lighter haired young man said, a bit sniffily, "Your army deserved to get hit with them, and I won't apologize for it."

"That would explain the decision to assault us with kitchen things, then, rather than swords?"

"Yes. You can't go about frightening the villagers."

"Apparently. I don't know who's dressed me down about it more -- you or my father."

"Anyhow, why did the ogres --"

"Don't ask. It leads down the path to madness."

"Ah."

The Fomorian that Reynaud saved, who had been hovering nearby, came closer and prodded Tom in the back with the handle of his double-headed axe.

"No more talk. Give us little yellow haired man! He attack us. We take blood price."

In a futile gesture, Reynaud the Black drew himself up to his full height. Though he was far from short, he was somewhat mortified to note that he was smaller than his entire army, as well as the woman he loved.

"I'll decide what is to be done with him! It's only because you disobeyed my orders that he went after you in the first place."

There were rumbles of dissent among the mercenaries.

"You let tall girl go when she step on us! We not say anything because she woman. Now you tell us set him free too?"

"Perhaps I shall!" he replied furiously, "I am your Commander, and you will do as I say! For the moment, the three of us are going to have a meeting in my quarters. You would do well to remember that I saved your life today!"

Without another word, Reynaud turned and led the other two humans to the black tent with the hedgehog flag. The soldiers said nothing as they passed. Once they were inside, however, many of the mercenaries, both ogres and Fomorians, spat on the ground in disgust.

"So, here we are again," the dark haired man said to Lady Topaz, filling her cup with wine, "What are we to do about all of this?"

They had settled comfortably in his tent, taking three of the four chairs around his dining table.

"I suppose the most obvious solution would be for me to go back to Swynmoor Castle with Lord Tomlin," she said, rather gloomily.

"About that," the lighter haired man said, "If you do return with me, Aunt Jilona has decreed that I'm going to marry you. To save your honor, since you've been in strange men's tents, you know."

"He isn't that strange," she protested.

"Nonetheless, I can rather see the old lady's point, as unpalatable as it may be," the darker haired man interjected.

"Reynaud -- do you still want to marry me?" she asked.

"As embarrassing as it is to have to say it in front of Moondown here -- yes, I seem to want that more each day."

"He did throw himself in between you and certain death by bread knife," said Tom.

"I don't know if it was certain death," the other man demurred, modestly, "But really, Lady Topaz, however much I may wish to spend my life with you, I simply couldn't bear for my desires to cause so much harm. As it is, everyone will make the most dreadful assumptions. And it wouldn't only hurt you. None of your sisters or cousins would be able to find husbands. Respectable ladies would shun your mother and aunts --"

"I know what happens to girls who are disgraced," she interrupted, her eyes suddenly full of tears, "Just this past season, one of the unmarried debutantes got pregnant."

"All in all, it's probably best if I take you back to the castle again," Tom suggested, "I'll find some way to talk Aunt Jilona out of the idea that we should be hitched together for life, just because of a bit of magic gone awry."

Topaz began to cry unabashedly, great droplets running down her face.

"I know it has to be this way. It's only that I've ended up in Reynaud's tent twice -- where I belong. But I keep having to go back to Swynmoor Castle, which is one of the last places I should be. No offense, Tom," she added through her tears.

"None taken."

Reynaud stood and strode over to where the tall girl was sitting. Grasping her hands, he pulled her up, so that she was on her feet next to him.

"Dearest, when we're together again, it won't be in a muddy tent. I want to be able to bring you proudly into my own home."

With that, he took her in his arms, stood on his tiptoes and kissed her. The lighter haired man quickly turned his eyes away in embarrassment. He had to admit, though, that what little he'd allowed himself to see was nothing but incredibly romantic. Up until this moment, he'd assumed that the sight of Topaz towering over her beloved, as they were clasped in an embrace, would seem absurd to him. He'd rarely been so pleased to be wrong about anything. He gave them a few moments, feigning intense interest in topping off his own wine cup. When he looked over at them again, they were only holding hands.

"Well, I suppose we should be off, then?" he suggested, rather awkwardly.

Topaz and Reynaud laughed bravely, though Tom noticed that the tears hadn't entirely stopped falling from the girl's eyes.

6

When she returned from The Fox and Geese, Kerris had to walk up many flights of stairs with an uneven gait, because she had one shoe off and the other on. She wanted to stomp angrily all the way back to her room, but she couldn't because she would risk hurting her exposed foot on the uneven flagstones. She was furious at Lord Tomlin for persuading her to go to an inn on St. Cuthbert's Day, a time which was meant for giving thanks to God for the annual harvest. He'd been like a devil whispering in her ear, convincing her that she would be protecting Lady Topaz's virtue by taking part in such debauchery. She was equally outraged that Reynaud the Black had deviously taken advantage of her naiveté to ambush them all. For the rest of her life, Kerris would never be able to forget the terror she'd felt as she fled. Her escape from the ogres and Fomorians had been so narrow that she'd smelled their foul breath as they chased after her.

When it came down to it, however, she had to admit that the person she was truly infuriated with was herself. What had she been thinking, agreeing to dress up in an immodest costume and spend a holy day in a tavern? She'd always been curious about the people and things that lay beyond the walls of the abbey, but that was no excuse for hedonism. She resolved to ask God for forgiveness, then amend her behavior. As long as she was trapped in this castle, she would say her prayers, study diligently, and wait patiently for the day that she could go home. If she ever made it back to the abbey, she would content herself with staying behind its locked gates for the rest of her life. Many years from now, she would tell young Foundling girls the story of her adventure out in the world, but only as a cautionary tale.

Kerris entered the servant girls' room that she'd been staying in, firmly shutting and locking the door behind her. She took off the garishly colored costume, laying it out carefully on her bed so that it wouldn't suffer any further damage. Then, she changed back into the grey dress, white apron, and opaque black stockings that she'd been wearing when she arrived. Silently asking both God and the absent owners to pardon her, she rummaged through several of the servant girls' clothes chests until she found some sensible black shoes, which were only slightly too big for her. She planned to find out who her unwitting benefactor was, and later, send her compensation from the abbey, either in the form of money or a new pair of shoes. She arranged her hair in a single braid that started at the top of her head and ran neatly down the center of her back. The plain clothes and hairstyle would help to keep vain thoughts from clouding her judgment.

Just then, as if God was providing a demonstration of the type of thoughts she was supposed to avoid, an image of Lord Tomlin's boyishly smiling face flashed into her mind. He'd been so charming during the brief time she'd spent with him at The Fox and Geese, solicitously serving her first from the selection of meat pies he'd ordered. How Kerris had wished that she'd been taught any of the country dances that Lady Topaz was able to do so effortlessly! She'd looked so carefree and joyous, clapping and twirling with Lord Reynaud. Disgusted with herself, the Foundling girl smacked her forehead hard with the palm of her hand, hoping that the pain would jar her out of coming up with any more unworthy ideas. There could be no doubt that what happened at the inn had been meant as a lesson. It was up to her to be grateful for it and make sure that she learned from the experience.

Determined to do the right thing, she headed straight for the library. There was no sense in wasting the daylight that was left. She would use it to do some translating. When she reached the book-filled room, Kerris immediately sat down at the large table, where she'd previously left a few piles of reference material. With the help of two dictionaries, including the one that had been accidentally brought from the abbey, she'd already managed to finish translating a very beautiful poem from its original Old Reachian. She looked over the work that she'd done the day before, just prior to getting dressed in her costume. Now that the ink had dried, she noted with satisfaction that her penmanship had turned out very well on this project. It probably had something to do with the fact that the pens were of excellent quality at the castle, but she'd also been practicing a lot lately. She would be sure to take the translation with her to show her teachers when she went home.

She looked at the books that were spread out before her, wondering what she should work on next. She never had so many choices at the abbey. Usually, she'd just translated whatever passages the sisters told her would be useful for her studies. Suddenly, however, Kerris remembered that she had intended to decipher the words she'd said over the pickled peppers, before her journey to Swynmoor Castle. She sorted through a few piles of books that were on the table before she found the volume she was looking for. Luckily, it was the sort of text that had a permanently attached ribbon to use as a bookmark, and she'd used it to remind herself where the ancient spell could be found. Locating an Old Reachian dictionary among the many volumes that were literally at her fingertips, she placed a fresh sheet of paper on top of her completed poem and set to work.

Kerris found herself scratching her head quite a few times as she struggled with the centuries-old language. This spell seemed to be older than she'd originally assumed it was, stemming from an even more ancient version of Old Reachian than even the sisters usually studied. Alternately, an illiterate person who spoke one of the more obscure dialects could have persuaded a nun to write down exactly what he'd said to her, word for word. Whatever the reason, translating the spell turned out to be more difficult than she anticipated, and the last rose-colored streaks of daylight were fading from the window by the time she finished. Trying to make sure that the translated work made sense as a whole, she squinted against the impending darkness and read it from beginning to end. It said:

If thou darest eat of me
According to thy nature
Transformed shalt thou be.

The angry man shall burn like fire.
The vain man shall be much admired.
The greedy man shall have his desire.

But time shall reverse all these things.
Before the lark his night song sings,
The flying man shall lose his wings.

Thou shall be again
As thou once were.
Men shall be men
And birds just birds.

How strange, she thought. Kerris wondered if she'd gotten the translation quite right. As the sun continued its descent outside, she yawned and stretched, suddenly realizing how exhausted she was from her ordeal at the inn. She knew that the monks and castle staff would be gathering for supper in the servants' dining area, which was in a large, comfortable alcove in a corner of the kitchen. She briefly thought about joining them but decided she was just too tired. Besides, since she'd officially been set free from kitchen duties, the cook often gave her the evil eye when they ate together. And she was in no mood for Brother Eustace's seemingly unending gossip about the other residents of Swynmoor Castle. She suspected that he relished the lax atmosphere he was now able to enjoy, away from the monastery. The monks often had long periods of time when they were compelled to be silent. Here, he could talk as much as he liked, and he took advantage of this freedom as much as possible.

Kerris ignored the petulant grumbling of her stomach and went directly back to her room. Lighting one of the lamps that she now had in abundance, she noticed that the costume that she'd left on her bed earlier was gone. There was a note in its place, written in even better penmanship than her own. She picked it up and read it. The note said:

> *Taken for repairs*
> *--Waltham*

Well, that was one less thing she needed to worry about. She undressed and put on a nightgown she'd been using which, like her recently acquired shoes, belonged to one of the servant girls. Kerris had brought a few of the more lighthearted books from the library into her bedroom to leave on her nightstand. She liked to read in bed, something that she'd only been able to do on the sly at the abbey. She'd often secreted a book and a lamp under her covers to use after the nuns had gone to bed and were no longer checking rooms to make sure the Foundling girls were asleep. At the moment, however, she was too tired to read even the most amusing letters of the legendarily witty St. Illyra. Pity, she thought. As she blew out her lamp, she reflected that for each person in religious life, there were different things about it that were difficult to bear. For her, there was the prohibition against reading before she went to sleep. For Brother Eustace, it seemed to be the silence.

Hunger woke her the next morning, just as the sun was rising. Her stomach gurgled and rumbled like the ocean at high tide. Even worse, there seemed to be another storm threatening to roll in, so her entire right side, especially her shoulder, ached and twinged mercilessly. Groaning aloud with various bodily discomforts, Kerris splashed some cold water on her face from the room's wash basin and hurriedly got dressed. She desperately needed to get downstairs for breakfast, so that at least some of her pains could be assuaged. She was tempted to take the stairs two at a time, but she refrained because her shoes were now slightly too big for her feet.

When Kerris reached the servants' dining room, several covered bowls and platters had been set in the middle of the table, so that people could help themselves. Breakfast was a particularly informal meal for the staff of Swynmoor Castle, since they were required to get up at very different times, depending on their jobs. Food was usually available from first light to mid-morning. When she arrived, unsurprisingly, all three of the monks that had come with her to deliver the taxes were already seated at the table. At the monastery, they were required to rise with the sun and couldn't seem to break the habit of a lifetime, even though they could have slept later while they were away from home. As usual, the two younger men were listening to Brother Eustace, who was talking animatedly.

"Good morning, Brothers," Kerris said politely.

"God bless you on this day and many others to follow," the older monk replied by rote, scarcely pausing for breath before returning to his monologue.

She sat down and piously made a triangle with her thumbs and fingers, shutting her eyes to say a silent blessing over the food. When she finished and looked around again, she noticed one of the quieter monks smiling at her in approval. She took a wooden plate from the center of the table and began ravenously lifting the covers from dishes. Once again, there was sausage, since Lady Swynmoor had generously supplied them with it in great quantity when she'd arrived. There were also chicken eggs from the castle's coops, though no duck eggs, largely because no one could go afield to gather them. Finally, there was a sort of mush made from day-old bread that had been torn into pieces and generously coated in goats' milk, ginger and cloves. Kerris served herself a helping of each, then poured a mug of tea to go with her breakfast. She took a large bite of her eggs, allowing herself to listen to what Brother Eustace was saying, now that impending starvation had been averted.

"It will be in only three days' time! Imagine -- having to prepare for such a thing with so little notice! Why, it's been years since I've even officiated at a wedding --"

"Of course," one of the younger monks interjected, "That's usually a duty for priests."

"There are no priests to be found at the castle, and her ladyship is determined that there shall be no delays, not even so that the wedding can be performed properly in a church, with a priest to bless the union."

"Who's getting married?" she interrupted, just before bringing the cup of tea to her mouth.

"Haven't you heard?" the older monk asked, "The news was all over the castle last night. Lord Tomlin and Lady Topaz are to be married -- almost without delay."

Kerris spluttered, only saving herself from spewing tea everywhere by taking a particularly large gulp. She immediately began choking loudly, gasping for breath between each cough.

"It's only to be expected," one of the younger monks said, "The way that girl has been carrying on, of course Lady Swynmoor would want to marry her off as soon as possible."

The Foundling girl took a few deep breaths, managing to get her coughing under control.

"But the wedding will be in only three days?" she asked, incredulously.

"Well, that's just what I was saying! I don't know how Lady Swynmoor expects me to have a sermon ready for something as important as a wedding with so little time. I'll have to choose appropriate readings. Honestly --"

He pushed a piece of sausage fretfully around on his plate, muttering to himself.

Kerris felt as if an unseen fist had punched her squarely in the chest. Why was there suddenly so little air? The image of Lord Tomlin's face flashed into her mind again, but this time, it had a cruel, mocking expression. Of course he was marrying Lady Topaz. Noblemen's wives were always members of aristocratic families, not Foundling girls from the abbey. The nuns had even been forced to make up a last name for her after she'd been discovered on their doorstep as a baby. Nobody had the slightest idea about who her mother or father was. Besides, she'd sworn to herself only the night before that she was going back to the abbey as soon as possible, where she would remain for the rest of her days. Surely, she'd meant that, hadn't she? It was too sudden, a small voice in her head protested. Yesterday, she'd been at the inn with Lord Tomlin, just beginning to feel --

"Forgive me, Brothers," she said, standing up hurriedly, "I have to go."

'But, your breakfast," one of the younger monks protested.

She rushed out of the servants' dining area, practically running up the stairs in her need to get away. She briefly considered going back to her bedroom again, but the library was closer, and no one ever seemed to make use of the place but her. Kerris hurried into the quiet room, slamming the door behind her. She breathed deeply, trying to inhale as much of the deeply reassuring scent of books as she could. People were untrustworthy, she thought, but books would never betray you. She went over to the large table and laid her head on an open page of one of the larger volumes. Strands of hair that were rapidly escaping from her tight braid spilled out across the paper. She was determined not to cry.

Topaz squared her shoulders, determined not to cry. Lady Glynis, Lady Swynmoor, and her maid were all picking at the tall girl with their fingers and jabbing her with little seamstress' pins. They had gotten the servants to bring several trunks of old clothes down from the attics, and they were making her try on a series of increasingly ancient wedding dresses. Somewhat disturbingly, each of them had been worn by a previous

Lady Swynmoor who was now long dead. They were also laughably outdated and smelled of mothballs. Even worse, not one of them came close to being the right length for her. The longest of the gowns still showed nearly a foot of exposed stocking.

Tom's aunt made a disapproving clicking noise with her tongue after each one was lowered over the girl's head, a sound which was invariably accompanied by the excited barking of several dogs. She and her maid would then turn the tall girl this way and that, as if they were trying to find an angle at which her height was less troublesome. At last, Lady Swynmoor would throw her arms up in disgust, and the process would begin over again with the next gown in the trunk. Tom's mother seemed to have given up entirely on the prospect of finding an appropriate wedding gown. Instead, she was focused on inserting an increasingly absurd series of objects into the girl's already elaborate hairdo. So far, there were feathers, bejeweled hairpins, live and silk flowers, and even a tiny model ship. Topaz looked as if she'd been the unfortunate victim of an explosion at a millinery shop.

"This simply will not do!" Tom's Aunt Jilona pronounced at last.

The maid began unlacing yet another bodice, which sat ridiculously high on the tall girl's chest.

"I could always add some lace to the bottom of one of the skirts, madam," she said, speaking awkwardly around a mouthful of pins.

"Even if you could fix the length of one of these gowns, the rest of it would still be ludicrously small."

"She could always wear her own best dress," Lady Glynis suggested, "It used to be what women did in the old days, before people got the idea that a wedding gown had to be worn just once."

"Honestly, I will not have the bride of my only nephew married in a dress that she's worn to tend the garden and walk the dogs!"

Several little dogs yapped emphatically, as if in agreement.

"We could delay the ceremony until I can get a proper dress," Topaz suggested, "Not to mention a priest, instead of a monk, and a real church. And I know that my mother would want to be here."

"Your mother would have wanted all those things for your wedding, but because of your behavior, you won't be able to have them! What she needs for you to have is an untarnished reputation!"

"But I didn't --"

"Now, Topaz, dear, let's not start again," Tom's mother interrupted, "Lady Swynmoor's complexion has scarcely recovered from last night."

There was a knock at the door.

"Just a moment," the maid called out.

Hurriedly, she finished getting the last of the ridiculously ill-fitting gowns off of the tall girl and wrapping her in a dressing gown.

"Come in," said Lady Glynis, when all of the numerous buttons and sashes had been done up.

The door opened, and Waltham stood there, a harried-looking messenger in tow behind him. Blinking, the old man took in the absurdity of Topaz's hair. It was only due to his decades of experience as a servant that he was able to turn his laugh into a discreet cough.

"Message for Lady Swynmoor," he said, after he'd finished with his sudden bout of choking.

"Good heavens, how did the man ever manage to get here with the House of Hedgehog blocking the castle in on all sides?" asked Tom's aunt.

"With all due respect, my lady, there are some letters that not even Reynaud the Black would keep from getting through," the messenger explained, rather solemnly.

"What on earth do you mean?" inquired Lady Glynis.

"Forgive me, but Lady Swynmoor will have to read it for herself."

He came a few paces forward to hand her a very official looking letter, which was sealed with a calligraphic letter "S" in blue wax. As she took it from his outstretched hand, he bowed and stepped back. A few dogs encircled his boots and began to sniff. As she broke the seal and unrolled the paper, complete silence descended, as if everyone was trying not to move a muscle until the apparently important news had been revealed. Her eyes scanned the page, then her hands began to shake, making the edges of the paper quiver. For the first time in anyone's memory, the proud woman began to drop to the ground in a faint. Her maid rushed to her side and caught her under the arms before her knees hit the floor.

"Jilona -- what on earth is it?" Tom's mother demanded.

"It's Malvern," she replied, in a small, rather detached voice.

"He hasn't decided to be foolish and risk the blockade to come here, has he?"

"He's dead," she replied.

Her eyes fluttered a few times, then closed completely. At last, her full weight became too much for the maid, and despite the girl's best efforts, her mistress' body sank down the rest of the way to the ground. There was a chorus of barking from the tiny dogs as all of them scurried over to her unconscious body. Many of them began licking her face and arms in a vain effort to revive her.

The next morning, it was a somber group of nobles who had gathered in the upstairs dining room for breakfast. All of them were wearing black, though Tom's aunt, as well as his reluctant fiancée, still managed to find dresses that were so busy they made his eyeballs ache, despite their drab colors. Even the dogs' collars had been changed to black ones that were studded with little diamonds. He wondered if Aunt Jilona had been storing them somewhere in the castle for years for just such an occasion. When he thought about it, he was rather surprised that she had left her room at all. The previous evening, several servants had been compelled to drag her back to her quarters in a dead faint, in which, it had been reported, she'd remained for many hours. It was the first time he'd laid eyes on her since she the news of his uncle's death had come. Despite some generously applied makeup, her face was decidedly gray.

"It's dreadful for you that Uncle Malvern has passed on," he said, kissing her on the cheek.

"Thank you, Tomlin, dear," she replied, "It has come as quite a shock."

"I'm sorry if this is too awful, but what are we going to do about a funeral?" Tom's mother asked, "Malvern's body is still in Finbarr Springs."

"Well, it is customary for bodies to be sent home by the fastest carriage possible," Aunt Jilona said, "It should be arriving in five days or so, if Reynaud the Black doesn't refuse it passage."

"Reynaud wouldn't do that," Topaz objected.

"Young lady, I am not at all certain that is the case. I am, however, hoping for the best."

A few of the family members began to help themselves to some food, but the recent widow stared resolutely at her empty plate.

At last she said, "I know that it would be a bit too early under the usual circumstances, but I believe I would like some brandy."

There was a flurry of people reassuring her that no one would think anything of it if she wanted a drink. A bell was rung, and a servant was soon dispatched to fetch her something considerably stronger than tea. After a large glass of brandy had been set at her place, for a few moments, there was no sound but the occasional metallic clink of someone's fork against a plate.

At last, Tom ventured to say, "I suppose this means the wedding will have to be postponed."

"It seems like the respectful thing to do," agreed the tall girl.

Lady Swynmoor, who had been taking a large swallow of her drink, set her cup down firmly.

"It absolutely will not," she stated emphatically, "Now that your Uncle Malvern has passed away, it is more crucial than ever that the Moondown line is assured."

"But we'll need to have a funeral," the young lord protested.

"Your uncle's body will not be arriving for at least five days. In case you've conveniently forgotten, your wedding was scheduled for two days from now. We shall have the marriage ceremony as planned. When your uncle returns home, we will have the funeral."

"But surely Malvern --" Glynis interjected.

"Malvern would have wanted it this way," she said with finality.

Topaz looked pleadingly across the table at Lord Tomlin, whose facial expression gradually changed from something approaching despair to grim determination. He stood up, grasping the edge of the table with both hands.

"Listen, Aunt Jilona, I'm sorry to have to do this sort of thing so soon, but --"

"What sort of thing could you possibly mean?"

"As I said, I hate to do this so quickly after Uncle Malvern has passed on, but you must realize that his death makes me the new Earl of Swynmoor."

"Everyone knows that," she said breezily, "I'll make certain that the monk addresses you by the appropriate title during the ceremony."

"Well, as the Earl, I'm entitled to all of the family's money. You can't threaten to withhold it any more if mother and I don't do what you say."

"Tomlin, dear, whatever are you babbling about?" she asked, her voice rising dangerously.

"And as the Earl of Swynmoor, I don't have to listen to you about when -- or even who -- I'm going to marry."

His aunt opened her mouth for what he assumed was an imperious retort, but no words came out. Her face reddened beneath the makeup, then she pressed her lips together again, apparently at a complete loss for words.

"Tom, dear!" his mother exclaimed.

"No, mother, I'm afraid there's nothing for it," he went on, "With all due respect to Lady Topaz, I'm officially declaring that the wedding is off -- for good."

"Nonsense," Tom's aunt replied at last, sounding slightly unsure of herself, "I promised the girl's mother that I would find a suitable match for her. Surely, you wouldn't --"

Topaz also stood and stared the old woman down coolly.

"I do feel sorry for your loss, and I would have waited until after the funeral service to tell you, if you hadn't insisted on going ahead with the wedding immediately," she began.

"Well, it seems that all the young people in the castle have been positively burdened with something they've been waiting to tell me until the moment I was widowed."

"My family won't have to worry about my being unmarried for much longer," she said.

For the first time since she'd read the letter, Tom's aunt smiled.

"You see, Tomlin, you won't get out of it so easily," she said gratingly, "That's right, dear, remind him it's his duty as a gentleman to save your reputation."

"Actually, Lady Swynmoor -- or I suppose it's Lady Jilona now -- I've been thinking about this for a while. I've decided that the only way I'll ever be happy is to leave this castle permanently. I'm going back to the encampment to marry Reynaud Evensea, if he'll have me."

The former Lady Swynmoor's smile rapidly faded, and she laughed bitterly.

"Surely not! You can't actually be standing before me, telling me that you're going to join yourself for life to the Noble House of Hedgehog! My dear girl, I must insist that you sit down immediately, and we'll all try to forget that you ever said such a foolish thing."

Lady Glynis interrupted, "But Topaz, dear, if you do this, your entire family will be disgraced! It will be terrible -- people will openly make fun of your sisters and aunts!"

"Yes, I'm certainly aware of that, which is why I returned to the castle in the first place. But the House of Fynchester is a perfectly respectable aristocratic family, and I'm sure that everyone will eventually get over the circumstances of my marriage into it. And if anybody has horrible things to say to my relatives for a while, I'm afraid I'll have little sympathy for them. For years, when I was mocked for my height, my entire family did nothing but constantly remind me about how terribly I'd embarrassed them. Now it will be their turn."

"Go then, you ungrateful girl!" Tom's aunt shouted, "Run to Reynaud the Black like a fool! But don't even think of coming back here crying when he only takes you for his mistress, then throws you into the gutter when he's through with you!"

All of the dogs that were under the table began yapping noisily, stirred up by her tone of voice. Everybody had to wait until the former Lady Swynmoor managed to quiet them down.

"Aunt Jilona --" Tom began, once canine pandemonium had been averted once more.

"No, it's all right," Topaz said, "She has a right to be angry, and she's very recently bereaved. I truly wish I didn't have to leave Swynmoor Castle on these terms."

Tom's aunt sniffed indignantly and looked away from the girl.

She went on, "I hope that some time, you'll find it in your heart to forgive me. But for the moment, I believe I should be going."

The tall girl pushed her chair back and left the upstairs dining room, thinking to herself that it might have been the most dignified exit she'd ever made from anywhere. It was much better than running away in disgrace because the entire court was laughing at her or having to flee because she was growing out of her clothes, anyhow. Without looking back, she went to her room and took off the black lace dress with all of its flounces, ruffles, and jewels. She ripped the bodice a little because she had to remove it without any assistance, but it didn't matter anymore. There was only one outfit that was appropriate for the occasion, and she changed into it -- the breeches and shirt of Reynaud the Black. She also took all of the absurd trinkets out of her hair, letting it fall naturally down her back. She looked in the mirror, nodding at her reflection with approval. Putting on her least fussy pair of shoes, she made her way to the stairwell at the rear of the castle.

As she closed the secret back door behind her, she noticed that someone was waiting for her outside. At first, she couldn't tell who it was because she was momentarily blinded by sunlight. Topaz wondered whether Lady Jilona had sent someone to bring her back by force. The figure came closer to her, and she tensed, undecided about whether she would try to fight or run away.

"Topaz?" the person's voice said in a very gentle tone.

The sun passed behind a cloud, and to her relief, she could now see that it was Tomlin.

"I don't suppose that you've been dispatched by your aunt to drag me kicking and screaming back to the castle, have you?" she asked.

"Right this moment, I'm afraid my Aunt Jilona doesn't want to see you ever again. Poor thing. It's been a simply wretched couple of days for her."

"If only she hadn't --"

"I know. She rather brought it on herself. That was the only way to stop the wedding, short of Reynaud showing up to crash the thing, accompanied by a dozen ogres and Fomorians, of course."

Topaz laughed, "It would almost have been worth going ahead with the ceremony, to see if he would do that."

"Aunt Jilona has no idea what we saved her from."

"So, why --"

"Am I standing here? Yes, well, I was getting to that. I wanted to, you know, wish you luck with the old chap. And I thought someone from our family should be polite enough to say goodbye."

"Thank you. It's nice to know that not everyone from the House of Swynmoor hates me."

"Good heavens, it's not as bad as all that. I don't even think that mother bears you any ill will. Aunt Jilona will buy a few more ridiculous dogs to assuage her wounded pride and move on."

"Speaking of moving on, I suppose I should really be off now."

"One more thing first?"

"Yes?"

"I wanted to give you something to remember your time at Swynmoor Castle by."

"Not that I think I could ever forget, but that's very kind of you."

"Close your eyes and hold out your hand."

She did as instructed and soon felt something in her palm that was a strange combination of soft strands interspersed with slightly sharp points. Curious, she opened her eyes and looked down. Much to her amusement, she saw Lady Jilona's now battered fake bird that had served as both a hair ornament and a prop for a pirate costume. She laughed out loud again.

"Thank you," she said, "I'll treasure it always."

"Naturally," said Tom, "Any girl would."

With that, he wandered off in the general direction of the front entrance of the castle, whistling.

Reynaud the Black was in his dark tent once again, lying on his back in bed and hoping that, at least for a few hours, he could get some peace. The day was off to a reasonably good start. There had been no letter from his father, and unlike yesterday, no messenger for Swynmoor Castle that he'd felt compelled to allow passage, for the sake of decency. But less than ten minutes after he'd retreated into his tent, leaving firm instructions with the mercenaries that he was not to be disturbed, the flaps rustled. An ogre's boar-like face peered through the narrow opening at him.

"For pity's sake, what is it?" he demanded.

"Tall girl is here," the ogre said.

"What on earth --" he began.

The black tent flaps parted further, and there was Topaz, dressed from head to foot in his clothes. He got up and immediately rushed over to her.

"Is everything all right? What are you doing here, dearest?" he asked.

"I'm back for good, Reynaud. I'm afraid I caused a scene at the castle, saying once and for all that I wasn't going to marry Tomlin because --" she broke off for a moment, blushing, "Because I'm in love with you."

"Truly?" he asked.

"I know we haven't known each other for very long, and I'm sorry if --"

Gently, he hushed her, putting his index finger to her lips. Reynaud cleared his throat and took both of her hands in his, which were surprisingly small for a girl of her height. He got down on one knee and looked up at her face, gazing deeply into her green eyes.

"Topaz Stonemont, will you marry me?" he asked.

As she'd been doing so often lately, the tall girl began to cry. But this time, there were only tears of joy running down her cheeks.

7

Kerris hadn't spoken to a soul since she'd found out that Tomlin and Topaz were soon to be married. She'd gone from the library to her bedroom and back again, nodding politely if she encountered a servant in the hallway. Although she'd left most of her breakfast untouched, she felt physically sick about the wedding and couldn't eat or drink for the rest of the day. She was almost faint from hunger and thirst the next morning, but she resolutely forced herself to wait until well after lunch to slip down to the larder. Avoiding people was far more important to her than even the loudest rumbling from the depths of her empty stomach. The entire castle would be buzzing with gossip about the marriage ceremony, and she simply couldn't bear to listen to any of it. For what must have been the hundredth time since she'd escaped from the mercenaries, she fervently wished that she could go home. She allowed herself one more sigh about being trapped in the castle, then made her way downstairs.

When she got to the kitchen, the cook was snoring peacefully in her customary chair beside the fireplace. Quietly, she took a wooden plate, mug and spoon from one of the many cabinets and stole past her into the smaller room where leftovers were stored. Kerris saw that, in order to give everyone a respite from seemingly unending meals of sausage, the old cook had apparently made a stew of salted cod and carrots for lunch. What remained of it was on one of the larder shelves, still cooling in a large wooden bowl, which had been covered with a napkin. She spooned the stew liberally onto her plate, then helped herself to a handful of almonds to accompany it. She briefly considered filling her cup with wine but, deciding that she wanted to keep a clear head, she got her drink from the ale keg instead. She was about to leave the larder when she caught sight of the barrels that she and the monks had brought.

It suddenly occurred to her that she hadn't even tasted this year's pickles. Resting her bowl on one of the other barrels, she pulled the stopper from the nearest one. A scent that was both vinegary and spicy wafted out of the opening. Definitely peppers, she thought. Her tiny fingers fit easily through the hole, and she pulled out several of the crunchy red vegetables. Wondering briefly if these were the ones she'd made, the Foundling girl replaced the cork and quietly made her way back upstairs. Not wanting to leave her work for too long, Kerris brought the food into the library. Taking a thoughtful drink from her mug, she stared down at her own precise handwriting, viewing the spell she'd finished translating the day before with a critical eye.

If thou darest eat of me
According to thy nature
Transformed shalt thou be.

The angry man shall burn like fire.
The vain man shall be much admired.
The greedy man shall have his desire.

But time shall reverse all these things.
Before the lark his night song sings,
The flying man shall lose his wings.

Thou shall be again
As thou once were.
Men shall be men
And birds just birds.

She'd checked both Old Reachian dictionaries several times to ensure that the translation was accurate. Taking a bite of the salty, somewhat mushy stew, she chewed reflectively. If the individual words were all correct, then what did they mean as a whole? Rather ruefully, she paused to rub her sore right shoulder with her left hand. The muscles on that side had been twinging from an approaching thunderstorm for two days now, and humidity had been hanging in the air like an ill omen. Whenever the storm got here, it was going to be huge. Perhaps the sky would open and pour on Lady Topaz's wedding. Kerris smirked for a moment, thinking of the perturbed look that the bride would have on her face. The Foundling girl's expression rapidly changed to a scowl as she silently chastised herself. Wishing bad fortune on others was a sin.

"According to thy nature, transformed shalt thou be," she read aloud, slowly.

Having just thought about Topaz, the image of her distressed face lingered in Kerris' mind as she said the words to herself. With her recent, mysterious growth spurt, she'd certainly been transformed, albeit briefly. The Foundling girl suddenly realized that it was stated in the spell itself that the changes wouldn't last very long. Excitedly, she read the words she'd written one more time. Yes, it all seemed to fit. Being taller than nearly everybody was certainly a quintessential part of the other girl's nature, however much she wished it wasn't. Going over everything she knew of the incident in her mind, Kerris remembered Tom saying that the girl had been at supper when she'd started to grow. Perhaps she'd eaten some of the enchanted peppers with her meal!

She stared at the pickles sitting on one side of her plate, seeming so innocent. When it came down to it, she didn't even know if they were from the same batch that she'd said the spell over. Cautiously, she prodded them with her finger, but they didn't seem unusual to the touch, any more than they were to look at. As she heard the rain beginning to patter on the rooftop of Swynmoor Castle, Kerris wondered what transformation she would undergo, if her theory was correct. She certainly wasn't tall, like Lady Topaz. The muscles in her shoulder suddenly stabbed her so mercilessly, she actually cried out in pain. She fervently wished that she'd find a spell one day that would free her from this misery.

She picked one of the red peppers up, holding it in front of her face with her thumb and forefinger. There was really only one way to find out if she'd somehow managed to cast an ancient spell on them. If it was possible that she'd inadvertently created magic pickles, it was her responsibility to sample them. For all she knew, the next person to eat some would be Lady Swynmoor, and she'd probably wreak havoc throughout the castle by turning into a larger version of one of the dogs she favored. Kerris repressed a giggle. Not giving herself any more time to change her mind, the Foundling girl dropped the pepper into her mouth and chewed. She swallowed it and waited for a few moments, but nothing unusual seemed to happen. Perhaps she hadn't created enchanted pickles, after all. Or maybe, she reflected, biting down on another one, these were from a different batch than the ones Topaz had eaten. Ominously, thunder rumbled loudly overhead as she swallowed the last of the second pepper.

The muscles down the entire right side of her body were suddenly suffused with pure agony. She fell off of her chair and writhed on the library floor, convulsing as if she'd been hit with lightning. Much to her surprise and relief, however, the torment was completely gone mere moments later, departing as rapidly as it had arrived. A sort of tingling had been left behind in its place. It coursed around, running up and down her side in circles, like water being stirred in a pot. She got to her feet, holding her side in what was probably a futile attempt to fend off any future attacks of pain. As she stood, Kerris was overcome with an inexplicable need to get closer to the storm. Almost immediately, this was tempered by the much more sensible desire not to get soaking wet. As if some unseen force had planted the thought in her mind, she remembered that there was supposedly a balcony on this floor. Going there would provide her with the shelter she needed overhead, while allowing her to still be outside. She began walking toward the place where the rain and thunder seemed to be summoning her.

Kerris' feet seemed to know exactly where to go, although she still regularly got lost in the castle when she wasn't going to the kitchen, her bedroom, or the library. She looked down in amazement at her sensible black shoes as they walked unerringly through the corridors, past rows of closed doors that seemed identical. At last, she turned a corner and saw the door that she instinctively knew was the right one. She grabbed hold of the knob, turned it and pulled. Although the doors at Swynmoor Castle were usually locked, this one opened without any resistance, as if it knew better than to defy the inexplicable power that was now inside of her. She walked through, and the wind blew it shut behind her.

"Come and play, Kerris!" the storm seemed to sigh in her ears.

As if it had a will of its own, her right hand held itself out in front of her chest and made a sweeping motion from side to side. Immediately, the wind picked up and swirled around the castle, making the gates below rattle against their chains. Experimentally, she raised her arm above her head, then flexed her hand back and forth at the wrist, as if she was waving. The storm responded by increasing the rain, pelting the castle with drops. Rapidly, she flicked three of her fingers outward, and lightning cracked into a tree that was standing on the castle grounds. It briefly burst into flame, which was quickly doused by the heavy rain. Taken aback by the fire, Kerris stopped controlling the storm long enough to appreciate the view from the balcony. She was astounded at how far she could see, despite the driving rain. She couldn't imagine how incredible everything would have looked on a clear day.

She gazed out further afield and saw the encampment of Reynaud the Black's army. It was spread out at the foot of the hill like a multicolored cluster of grapes. Stupid Lord Reynaud, she thought, with his devious ambush at The Fox and Geese that ruined everything. It was all because of him and his ridiculous army of ogres and Fomorians that she was trapped here. She couldn't go back to the abbey or even find a nearby place to hide from the impending wedding. Feeling anger building up inside of her body, she fixed her eye on one bright blue tent and made the sweeping motion with her hand again. As if it was a toy that had been kicked over by a petulant child, it turned over and blew away into the forest. She laughed out loud, feeling drunk with power. If they wouldn't leave of their own accord, she thought, she could send them as far away as she liked. The landscape would be uncluttered again, and she could go back to the nuns who had raised her. They, at least, had some affection for her, unlike anybody in the world beyond the abbey's walls. Throwing her head back, Kerris raised her arm above her head once more, this time willing the thunder to crack and boom like the sky was splitting.

Garrok and Izir ran frantically toward the tent of their Commander, their shouts drowned out by the nearly deafening sounds of the storm. When they got there, they found a note pinning the tent flaps closed. Without the slightest pause, the Fomorian general ripped it down and pulled the flaps open. He found that the palanquin was empty, and Reynaud the Black was nowhere to be found. Crying out wordlessly, the two generals rushed over to the tent of Jack, the Commander's manservant. He was their only hope of finding someone in the camp who could read. Frantically, the ogre tore open the entrance of the other human's smaller tent. Unlike his master, this man was there.

"Jack!" yelled the Fomorian, thrusting the note at the startled man, "You help now! Read!"

Puzzled, he took the crumpled piece of paper from Izir's large, warty hand. Quickly, he read it over, then looked up at the anxious mercenaries, an expression of astonishment on his face.

"It says the Commander's gone into the village with that tall girl to get married!" he announced.

Both of the mercenaries groaned aloud wordlessly.

"This is a bad storm! Very bad!" Garrok shouted, "When it is like this at home, we go very deep into the cheese caves!"

"No cheese caves here! No tunnels! What we do?" Izir demanded.

Jack sighed. He was beginning to see why Lord Reynaud looked so pained all the time.

"I don't think we have any choice but to make our way to Swynmoor Castle. Perhaps they'll have pity and take us in."

Both of the mercenaries nodded enthusiastically.

"Yes. Good plan, Jack," the ogre pronounced.

"Of course Lord Reynaud would be away at a time like this," the manservant muttered.

A few hours before, almost as soon as the word "yes" had escaped from Topaz's trembling lips, Reynaud the Black swung into action. Throwing a few items that he'd deemed necessary into a saddlebag, he grabbed the tall girl by the wrist, briefly leaned over her hand to kiss it, and pulled her out of the tent.

"Where are we going?" she asked.

"Well, my love, you do want to marry me, correct?"

"Of course!"

"Unfortunately, your marriage to another man is still immanent unless we act quickly and decisively. I'm sorry that you won't be able to have the wedding that little girls tend to dream of, but we need to have the legalities dispensed with as soon as possible. If you like, we can have another ceremony, complete with all the flowers and bells, once we get to Fynchester."

"So we're going to find a priest to marry us before anyone from Swynmoor Castle can come looking for me?" she asked.

"Brilliant, as well as beautiful! I knew I chose the ideal woman!" he said, without the least hint of sarcasm.

Suddenly, the dark haired man stopped, mid-stride.

"Wait here for a moment, will you, dearest? I suppose I really should leave a note."

Cursing under his breath, he squelched through the mud back to the tent with the hedgehog flag flying above it. Topaz watched as he went back inside for a few minutes, then emerged to pin a piece of paper to his closed tent flaps. He nodded, then hurried back to her side.

"Now, where were we?" he asked, a bright grin on his face.

"I believe we were eloping," she answered, just as cheerfully.

"Right. Let's get on with it, then, shall we?"

He guided her to a field, where several horses, as well as two rather frightening looking bicorns, were grazing. He whistled, and a black steed immediately raised his head from the grass he was cropping to look over in their direction.

"Come on, Altairos," he called.

The horse trotted over to them, whinnied, and lowered his head for a scratch behind the ears. Reynaud complied, rubbing and petting the animal's head.

"Horses," he said, shrugging.

Their mount was soon saddled up and ready to go. Reynaud got onto Altairos' back and pulled his near-future wife up behind him. She was quite pleased to find that she could ride astride now, since she was wearing trousers. Somewhat to her surprise, the journey to Swynmoor Village went seamlessly. They even managed to make it to the edge of town before the first raindrops began to fall.

The young lord said, "It looks as if it's going to rain on our wedding day."

"I'm not superstitious," replied the tall girl.

"Neither am I," he stated, urging Altairos to go a bit faster.

It wasn't difficult to find the church, since it was, by far, the tallest building in the village. Threading their way through the narrow, unpaved streets, Topaz noticed the shocked looks on the villagers' faces as they passed. Many of the women abruptly stopped whatever they were doing, grabbed hold of their children, and retreated into their houses. One red-haired young mother dropped the water jug she'd been holding, allowing the vessel to shatter on the ground in her haste to pick up her little boy and get inside.

"These people are afraid of you, Reynaud," the tall girl said.

"That would be due to the fearsome reputation that my father insisted that I create for myself. Well, that and the fact that I raided the village recently with my army to steal cookware."

"I'd forgotten about that. Why did you say you did it again?"

"I never did say. And it's best not to ask. As I told Moondown, that way lies madness."

She nodded sagely, although he couldn't see her doing it, since he was in front of her on the horse.

"You're obviously with me, so they're going to be scared of you too," he warned, "Especially since you're dressed in black, my official color, from head to foot. Are you still sure you want to marry me?"

"That will never change," she said, tightening her grip on his waist.

"I suppose that's for the best, then, since we're coming up on the church."

It rose before them, red brick spires reaching up into the sky. Although it was the grandest building in the area, it was still a simple village church, nowhere near as elaborate as the ones that either of them had grown up with in their respective homes. Over the years, wind and weather had knocked some of the tiles on the roof wildly askew. Still, there would be priests inside that could marry them, so as far as Topaz was concerned, it was more than adequate for their needs. The dark haired young lord dismounted, helped her to get down, and then tied Altairos to the hitching post that had been installed at the side of the steps. Raindrops began to fall in earnest, causing the horse to flatten his ears and look at Reynaud somewhat accusingly. He patted the animal, then rummaged briefly through the saddlebags. Finding what he wanted, he pocketed it and took the tall girl's hand once again. The two of them rushed up the stairs and through the doors, narrowly escaping getting quite wet.

Once inside, they could see two men, one wearing black robes and the other dressed similarly in brown. On their knees, they were attending to the lit prayer candles that had been placed on the floor near the altar by parishioners. They righted and relit the ones that had fallen over and placed bits of paper under any that were dripping wax onto the ground. Almost simultaneously, they looked up from their work when they heard the sound of heavy boots echoing loudly on the flagstones. At the sight of Reynaud the Black striding rapidly down the aisle, accompanied by a very imposing looking woman, the man in brown cried out and dove behind the altar. Thunder began growling melodramatically overhead as they approached.

"Angels preserve us!" shouted the one in black robes, "Take whatever you want, but I swear we don't have any pots and pans!"

"Are you a priest?" the dark young man asked, gruffly.

"Excuse me?"

"Are you a priest? A man of God?"

The one in brown poked his head out from behind the altar to point at the other person.

"That man is," he declared, "I'm just a brown-robe. Still in training, you know."

"Excellent," Reynaud said.

He gently nudged the extremely tall young woman, who was strangely dressed in men's clothing, toward the one who had been identified as a priest.

"You can marry us. That one," he said, nodding in the general direction of the altar, "Can serve as the witness."

"Then, you haven't come to steal from us?"

"Good heavens, man! I admit to taking some cookware, but I wouldn't rob a church! What do you take me for? In fact --"

To the mutual alarm of the two holy men, the dark haired lord reached into one of his pockets. They were relieved to see that all he pulled out was a leather purse, which he tossed toward them. It landed on the stone floor, jingling slightly. Hesitating somewhat, the priest stood up and came forward a few steps. He looked up at Reynaud, and when he nodded, the black-robed man took hold of the purse and picked it up. He untied the leather cords that held it closed and gazed inside. Almost instantly, his face seemed to light up in wonder.

"See that whoever was robbed by my army gets compensated. Handsomely. You're a priest, so I assume I can trust you with money. There should still be enough left over for you to fix the roof and feed some hungry people."

"Bless you, m'lord!" the priest exclaimed, "I -- I'm certain that God will forgive you for the robbery, since you seem to have amended your life."

"Now, on to the next matter of business. This young lady and I wish to be married immediately."

"Married? Oh, yes! Certainly, Lord Reynaud. Let me get my psalter, and I'll see to it."

"Thank you very much," said the extremely tall girl.

The priest looked over toward the altar, then shook his head.

"For pity's sake, Hubert, you can come out now. It's perfectly safe," he called out.

Hesitantly, the other man poked the top half of his head up, peering out as if someone was shooting arrows at him.

"Are you sure?" he asked.

"Yes, yes. Besides, as the good man said, you're going to have to serve as the witness for this marriage ceremony."

At that moment, thunder crashed particularly loudly overhead.

"I say, before the wedding gets underway, is there anywhere indoors where I can stable my horse?" asked Reynaud.

Struggling against the wind, Jack led his horse, as well as the army of mercenaries, up the hill toward Swynmoor Castle. The rain pounded down without surcease, and at times, the wind actually blew him back a few paces. Rearing and screaming with terror, all of the steeds had to be led, since they were far too skittish to be ridden. The battered group trudged through the storm on foot, with the exception of the two generals. They were able to ride because their mounts were sturdy black bicorns, which were determined not be frightened by something so beneath their notice as a storm, no matter how big it was. Holding the reins of his grey animal, Jack turned to look curiously back at the encampment.

Individually and in pairs, the tents were collapsing under the force of the wind and being blown into the forest. To the manservant, they looked like huge, brightly colored bats swooping backward across the sky. Shaking his head, he turned his face toward the castle again, his normally perfectly groomed bangs blowing into his eyes with the force of the gale. Suddenly, he felt himself being lifted off of his feet. Fortunately, the horse planted his hooves, while Jack avoided being blown away by continuing to hold fast to the reins, no matter how painful it became. He shouted with relief when the wind let up enough for him to get his feet firmly on the ground again. He had suffered deep cuts in his palms -- the price of hanging onto the leather straps. Swallowing hard, he patted the steed gratefully with a bloody hand and continued on in the face of the tempest. As the member of the group who, by far, weighed the least, Jack knew that he was in the greatest danger from the storm. Why, he thought, had Lord Reynaud left him alone with the ogres and Fomorians today, of all days?

From the balcony, Kerris watched tents being swept away in the storm, her storm, and laughed out loud. A small part of her mind was insisting that she would feel terrible if anyone got hurt, or worse, killed because of her. An even more miniscule part was aware that her conscience would be considerably louder tomorrow, drowning out even the happiness she would feel about finally being able to go home. For the moment, however, there was only rain and wind, thunder and lightning. She controlled it all, like a conductor of some sort of meteorological orchestra, instructing the gales to blow over here and bolts of fire to strike over there.

She'd noticed the band of Fomorians and ogres struggling up the hill in a rather vain attempt to escape from the weather, but for the moment, she felt no pity for them. Chase her out of The Fox and Geese, would they? Well, she'd show them.

Unfortunately, however, she felt a growing sense of awareness that her abilities were on the wane. She had to concentrate harder and make broader hand gestures to get the wind to blow tents away, and now she was only able to summon up distant thunder that didn't sound threatening at all. She also couldn't deny that the current of power in her body was steadily decreasing. Soon, it would be gone, and she'd go back to being just a Foundling girl that nobody, including her own parents, had ever really wanted. Kerris decided that it was time to go to the larder again. She would find the barrel of pickled peppers, eat twice as many, and become an even stronger Lady of the Tempest. She allowed her right arm to drop to her side and turned toward the door.

"Don't leave us, Kerris," the storm implored.

No need to worry, she thought -- I'll return in a few moments. When I come back, the loudest voice in her head continued, if I feel the least desire to do it, I'll be able to tear Swynmoor Castle apart with blasts of wind or even set it on fire with a lightning strike. She opened the door, intent on getting to the pickles as quickly as possible. However, as soon as it closed behind her, and she was standing in the corridor again, her entire right side was permeated with white hot agony. The force of it made her drop to the floor with overwhelming pain. She screamed, clutching her side with her left hand, and then everything went black.

Jack had reached the gates of Swynmoor Castle and was rattling them frantically, desperately hoping that someone inside would hear, when the howling of the wind abruptly stopped. He looked up at the sky, waiting to see whether this was some cosmic trick, and the heavens were simply pausing before unleashing another onslaught. The ogres and Fomorians on all sides of him (except, of course, in front, where there was nothing but castle) were doing the same. The thunder and lightning also seemed to have finished wreaking havoc, and while rain continued to fall, it was simply a steady downpour, not the deluge they had been experiencing. Piously, he made a triangle with his thumbs and fingers, grateful that God had, at last, seen fit to spare them. Similarly, many of the mercenaries raised their arms up, palms spread to the sky, in a gesture of thanks to their respective deities.

"Gods have forgiven us," said Izir.

Having gotten Altairos safely stabled in unexpectedly nice quarters, as far as accommodations for horses went, Reynaud proceeded to marry Topaz. It was a very small, but definitely legally binding, wedding. After the service, they had planned to head back to the encampment immediately, but they found themselves delayed by what seemed to be the mother of all storms.

"Is this normal in these parts?" he asked the holy men.

"Gracious, no," said the priest, "I've lived here all my life and never seen anything like it. You'd better stay for a while to wait this one out."

Accordingly, the four of them went down into the basement of the church. There, Topaz discovered a great deal of fresh bread and wine that had been stored for use in future religious services. Fortunately, the priest was able to determine that it hadn't been sanctified yet and could be consumed with impunity. It seemed that the most sensible thing to do under the circumstances was to have something of an impromptu celebration. So, the new bride and groom had a merry time enjoying a very simple wedding feast with the priest and priest-in-training, while the tempest raged outside. By the time they were able to emerge several hours later, they were all rather drunk. Embarrassingly, Hubert expressed zeal for certain aspects of married life that was rather unbecoming for someone who professed a calling to the priesthood. Reynaud got Altairos saddled rather quickly, before the younger of the two holy men had a chance to say something that he would probably regret when he was sober.

"Thank you very much," the newlyweds called out from the horse's back.

"You have a good time tonight," the brown-robed man enthused, "Reynaud, if you ever want to come back and tell me all about how you like being married -- ow!"

"God bless you, my children," the priest interrupted, his foot firmly on top of the other man's, "Travel safely."

Topaz turned and waved at them as the steed began picking his way through the narrow streets once again. As they rode, the newlyweds couldn't help but notice that the village had suffered some damage in the storm. Laundry that had been hanging out to dry was scattered onto the tops of houses. Thatched roofs were thoroughly soaked on some people's homes, while tiles had been blown off of other ones. Portions of quite a few fences had been knocked down. The wooden sign for The Fox and Geese dangled precariously, hanging on by only one of the four chains that normally kept it attached to its pole. A child's shoe tumbled deliriously along the side of the street, set free from its tiresome duties at last. A window's shutters opened as they went past, and a woman's face emerged. She extended a hand out, palm upraised, presumably to check if it was still raining. Catching sight of Reynaud and his new wife, she huffed indignantly and slammed the shutters closed again.

"You know," the dark haired man said, "I wouldn't be surprised if the villagers found some way to blame me for all of this."

"Your father would probably be rather pleased if they did," she consoled him.

"I suppose there is that," he sighed.

The closer they got to the encampment, the more damage from the storm there seemed to be. Branches littered the road, and from time to time, they noticed that entire trees had been blown down. One of them was blocking the road enough that the young lord had to dismount and strain every muscle he had to push it out of the way. Curiously, they began seeing large, brightly colored pieces of fabric caught in the tops of trees that had staunchly managed to remain upright.

"What on earth --" began Topaz.

"I hate to tell you this, my love," her husband interrupted, "But I believe those are what little remains of my army's tents."

When they reached the camp site, there was no escaping the fact that it had been utterly destroyed. Not a single tent was standing, and everything from axe-handles to the ill-fated pots and pans had been strewn everywhere. They each dismounted and looked around, their eyes wide with disbelief.

"It's as if the storm was sent by God specifically to ruin this place," Reynaud said, his voice flat with shock.

As if drawn to it, the tall girl walked rapidly over to a spot on the ground. She crouched down, fished something out of the mud, and triumphantly raised a hand over her head, holding the object tightly in her grasp. It was the hedgehog banner of the House of Fynchester, which looked only slightly the worse for wear.

"Not everything was lost," she said, smiling, "I must really be a member of your family now. I knew exactly where to find it."

"I suppose that hedgehog is tougher than I imagined," he replied, "It managed to survive one Hell of a storm. It might actually do all right in battle."

Reynaud looked up in the direction of Swynmoor Castle to determine whether it had sustained any damage that was obvious enough that he'd be able to see it, even from this distance. To his surprise, what he saw instead was a wet, bedraggled army of ogres and Fomorians making their way toward him, their steps agonizingly slow with exhaustion. Oddly, his manservant, Jack, accompanied by his grey horse, seemed to be leading them all. Both mercenary generals were just behind him, mounted on their fearsome black bicorns. Not wanting to make them walk any further than they had to, he ran toward them. There was only one of him, and he was considerably more rested, so he was able to get to them quickly. They all stopped gratefully when they got close enough to their Commander that they could speak to him. He could see that the bicorns were dripping a great deal of water from their shaggy manes.

"Merciful heavens!" he cried, taking in the sight of the ragtag group, "You all look dreadful!"

"Thank you, sir," his manservant replied ruefully.

"I didn't mean --" he began.

"Commander, we have to tell you something," Garrok interrupted him.

"Gods angry. They make giant girl. They make pots and pans that hit. They send storm," said Izir.

"Surely you don't think --" the dark haired man began.

"We will not defy the gods," the ogre continued, "We will not fight for you any more. We are sorry, but we are going home."

There was general nodding and sounds of assent from the rest of the troops. Reynaud opened his mouth to argue, but for the life of him, he couldn't think of any reason why he really should. He had never wanted this war to begin with. All he felt like doing was taking his new bride back to Fynchester and living peacefully with her for a very long time.

"Yes," he agreed, "We should go home."

Kerris awoke somewhere that was considerably more comfortable than anyplace she'd ever slept before in her entire life. Eyes still closed, she stretched, wondering where she was. Feeling a slight twinge of pain in her right shoulder, memories of what had happened after she'd eaten the pickled peppers came flooding back to her. Hopeful that it had all been a dream, she opened her eyes at last. She saw that Lord Tomlin was in the room with her, thankfully completely dressed and sitting in a chair next to the bed. Panicked, she looked under the sheets to make sure that she wasn't naked. Much to her relief, she found that her body was fully clothed.

"Ah, you're awake," he said cheerfully, "I hope you don't mind that Waltham put you in my bed to recover. It was quite a lot closer than yours."

"What happened?" she asked.

"It was rather odd, really. One of Aunt Jilona's dogs found you passed out in the corridor after that ruddy enormous storm. It started barking like billy-o, and Waltham went to see what was the matter."

"Shouldn't you be with Lady Topaz?" she asked, rather coldly, "I'm sure that the tempest was quite upsetting for her."

"Why on earth would I be taking care of her? That's Reynaud's job now. For the rest of his life, I'd expect."

She looked confusedly at him. Having just awoken, she wasn't able to formulate the words she needed.

"Hang on," he added, "I suppose you may not have heard about that. You've locked yourself up in the library, ever since we got back from that dreadful business on St. Cuthbert's Day. Topaz ran off to elope with Reynaud. I'd suppose that they're man and wife by now."

Kerris sat up so quickly that she cracked the top of her skull painfully on the headboard.

8

Tomlin asked one of the servants to bring Kerris some tea, and despite her throbbing shoulder, she managed to prop herself up on the voluminous pillows. While she sipped the welcome hot drink, the young lord told her what had been happening while she'd been locked away in the library. Her heart briefly swelled with happiness when she heard about the abruptly cancelled wedding -- a feeling that was immediately quashed by a thought that filled her with shame. Everything she'd done while she had power over the storm had not only been destructive, it had also been completely unwarranted. Lord Reynaud never betrayed them, and Topaz had quite efficiently dispensed with the marriage that no one wanted, other than Lady Jilona. It was interesting, of course, to hear about what happened to the new Earl of Swynmoor after he'd eaten some of the enchanted peppers, although he had no idea why he'd briefly possessed the ability to control metal. The Foundling girl did not enlighten him. There was only one person she intended to tell about the pickles, and it wasn't Tom. After the pain her shoulder had truly subsided, she thanked him for the tea and the use of his bed. Once she'd reassured him that she really was all right, she went in search of Brother Eustace.

Although monks and nuns were devoted to the same God, Kerris knew that they sometimes disagreed about what He required of them. The men generally felt that anything which remotely seemed like magic was evil, but the sisters, almost by necessity, took a considerably more broad view. It was the nuns who had been tasked with translating ancient texts, many of which were of pagan origin. Books by authors with polytheistic beliefs sat quite contentedly in their libraries next to volumes penned by long-dead saints. They often encountered old spells in the course of their work. Furthermore, village women usually came to the abbey when it was time to deliver their babies. The sisters were not above using magic to keep mothers and children from dying, especially when it was the best tool for the job. Kerris understood that after her body's sensitivity to weather manifested, she might have had quite a different childhood indeed if she'd been a boy being raised by monks.

The Foundling girl took no chances with telling anybody about the pickles who might decide to keep them around "just in case". She found Brother Eustace in the kitchen and, after asking to see him privately, she eventually managed to get him to stop talking about the cancelled marriage ceremony. Once she was able to get a word in edgewise, she told him about the enchanted peppers and all the trouble they'd been causing. He gravely agreed when she suggested that they should be gotten rid of in secret, before somebody else ate one. As far as he was concerned, no good ever came from having anything magic around.

In the dead of night, after nearly everyone in the castle was asleep, the Foundling girl showed the monks which barrel contained her pickles. With as much stealth as they could manage, the three of them loaded it onto one of the carts they'd driven to Swynmoor Castle. Under cover of darkness, they made their way to the nearest river. (Unbeknownst to them, it also happened to be the one that Reynaud's mercenaries had thrown the cookware into.) The holy men hacked the barrel open with an axe and dumped its contents into the rushing water, which bore the magic peppers to wherever the pots and pans had gone. For good measure, they heaved the barrel itself into the river after its contents. They watched it float away on the current, making triangles with their thumbs and fingers after it finally bobbed out of sight. If any fish briefly acquired magic powers after that night, no humans ever told the tale. The monks arrived at breakfast the next morning with dark circles under their eyes, but Brother Eustace was able to nod definitively at Kerris when she gave him an inquiring look.

Reynaud the Black's mercenaries were far too busy packing up what little they could salvage from the storm to offer any challenge to the passage of the deceased Malvern Moondown's carriage. Having heard that it was safe to return at last, the staff of Swynmoor Castle also began to make their way home. By ones and twos, each day more servants returned, and even the few guards that the family had been able to afford came back. The kitchen staff was soon put to work making food for guests who were already arriving for the interment services. Having been denied the wedding ceremony she wanted, Lady Jilona made up for it by throwing a truly elaborate funeral for her husband.

Although tradition compelled Tom's aunt to dress in somber colors, she summoned a seamstress to make her a widow's dress with copious amounts of black jewels, ruffles, and fabric flowers. When the day of the former Lord Swynmoor's burial arrived, she could barely walk down the aisle of the church, due to the sheer weight of her clothing. The dogs did an admirable job of lining up on either side of the coffin like a tiny, furry honor guard, and not even one of them yapped during the service. Nobles had arrived from all over Highreach to console the bereaved family, and even the queen herself put in a brief appearance at the gravesite. There was a particularly sumptuous feast afterwards, since Lady Jilona had arranged for each region's local delicacies to be imported for the funeral supper. Much to the relief of Tom's mother, everything was expertly cooked by the recently returned servants.

For the sake of politeness, Kerris and the monks stayed at Swynmoor Castle until after the interment was over. The Moondowns had played host to them for quite a while, and it wouldn't have been right to dash off in the family's hour of need. Besides, there were lots of interesting people around for Brother Eustace to talk with, and he knew he probably wouldn't be afforded such an opportunity again. At last, after many of the funeral guests had gotten back on the road, it was time for the Foundling girl and the monks she'd come with to go home. Although Kerris had previously been desperate to leave, it was with decidedly mixed feelings that she packed her few belongings, including the books she'd accidentally brought from the abbey. She was placing some of the other volumes she'd been using back on the shelves, when there was a knock at the library door.

"Come in," she called.

It opened, and the recently elevated Lord Swynmoor, looking a bit sheepish, stepped into the room. He was dressed all in black and holding a rather silly-looking hat. She was certain that his aunt had gotten it made for him.

"Hello, Kerris," he said, twisting the hat nervously in his hands.

"It's very kind of you to stop by."

"Well, it wouldn't do for you to leave without a word from me. You've been around long enough that it almost feels like you're part of the family now."

"You flatter me. If anything, it probably seems to you more like I'm a member of your staff."

"About that, actually. I just wanted to let you know that -- well, you don't have to go. You could stay on and sort out the castle's library. I'm sure the old place could use it, and of course, I'd pay you some sort of reasonable salary, though I'm not sure what the going rate is for librarians."

Kerris nearly dropped the book she was holding. Carefully, she put it back where it belonged before turning to look the young lord squarely in the eye. He had a pleading expression on his face, as if it was truly painful for him to let her leave. She had to admit, at least to herself, that his offer was quite tempting. The library at Swynmoor Castle was considerably bigger than the one at the abbey, and she could work here without any of the sisters perpetually looking over her shoulder. She was also still quite curious about the world, however fraught with temptations she'd found it to be. And there was always the draw of Lord Tomlin himself. But something in her heart knew that if she was ever going to leave the abbey, it would have to be under different circumstances indeed.

"That's so kind, Lord Swynmoor --" she began.

"For heaven's sake, do call me Tom!" he said, too emphatically.

"Yes, of course --" she corrected herself, sounding flustered.

"Forgive me, I didn't mean to shout. It's just that I haven't suddenly become a different person because my uncle died, but everyone's been treating me as if I have. It's all been terribly confusing."

"I'm sorry you've been finding your new responsibilities troubling. I wish I could stay to help, but I think I'd also find it difficult to suddenly have such a different life."

"I'm certain you'd get used to it. It isn't so bad, you know, being here."

"I'm sure there would be much to like about it. To be honest, though, I've done some things since I've been at the castle that I'm not proud of. I need to work out why I did them and whether I'd really be able to be a good person if I was away from abbey for good."

"Will I ever see you again?"

She smiled, and her amber eyes were so sharply beautiful that they seemed to pierce Tom's heart.

"I'm allowed to spend time with people every Saturday in the visitors' area. If you came to call, we could walk in the gardens, and I could show you our chapel. I've never had anybody visit before, since I'm a Foundling, but --"

"That sounds marvelous! Of course I'll come -- every week, if you'll let me! Swynmoor Abbey isn't exactly far away, and we could always write during the rest of the week, couldn't we?"

She giggled, "Yes, we do get letters. Sometimes, we even send them, too."

He strode over to her, took her hand, and gallantly raised it to his lips.

"For now, I bid you goodbye with a much less heavy heart. Do remember that the job will always be open, if you change your mind."

"You wouldn't hire another librarian?" she asked innocently.

"Never. You're the only one for the job."

Tom made his way back through the hallways of the castle that was now truly his. Despite the fact that he was officially still in mourning, he was in a decidedly good mood. Whistling his way through the corridors, he decided to stop off at his aunt's sitting room to see how she was holding up. He knocked politely, and a torrent of barking ensued.

"Who's there?" his Aunt Jilona's voice demanded imperiously.

"It's Tomlin, your worthless nephew," he replied, smiling.

"Tomlin? I suppose you'd better come in."

He happily sauntered through the door. Much to his surprise, however, he found his aunt's sitting room in complete disarray. Several servant girls were hurrying about packing suitcases, and bits of ridiculously frilly women's clothing seemed to be everywhere. A pair of black silk stockings hung over the back of her favorite chair, and one of her high heeled shoes, which was covered in filigree buckles and studded with jewels, was lying on the floor. He saw that his mother was also there, her perpetual look of worry fixed firmly on her face.

"What on earth is going on?" he asked.

"I didn't know how to tell you this, dear, but your Aunt Jilona and I are going to Finbarr Springs."

"Why would you --"

His aunt interrupted, "Well, you've certainly made it known that my advice is not wanted here. And in truth, I've found it rather difficult to get used to life as a widow. I thought it would be best to return to a place where I could take the waters."

"But surely you're not going as well, are you, mother?"

"I can hardly allow your poor aunt to go by herself. She'd be lonely. Besides, I might be able to help her with learning how to be on her own. I know it seems like your father's been gone for a long time, but it wasn't so many years ago that I was bereaved myself."

"And I thought I might finally buy Glynis some fashionable clothes. The dresses that she's been going about in -- really!"

Several dogs barked, as if in agreement.

"But you're just going to leave me here?" he asked, unhappily.

His aunt sniffed, "I tried to get you married to an appropriate bride, but you simply wouldn't hear of it. Now you shall have to figure out how to manage Swynmoor Castle on your own. I can only hope that you won't make too much of a pig's dinner of it!"

"You'll be all right," Lady Glynis reassured him, "The servants are back now, and most of them have worked here their entire lives. I'm sure that Waltham will be able to give you plenty of good advice, if you need it."

"Of course, you should do what you think is best," he sighed, "But honestly, mother, I'm not entirely sure what I'll do without you."

"I know, dear. We've hardly been apart since you've come back from school. But you're a young man now. I trust you to make the right decisions."

"Have a good journey, then. Don't forget to write when you get there, so I'll know you've arrived safely."

"Just listen to the boy!" Tom's aunt exclaimed, "How many years have I implored him to send letters to me regularly? And now --"

"Don't worry, Aunt Jilona. I'll write to you, as well."

Kissing each of his female relatives on the cheek, the young lord turned and went back into the hallway. He could go anywhere he liked now, he realized, which was not a state of affairs he was used to. How strange it was not to have anybody making demands on his time! He was about to head to the armory, when he noticed Waltham approaching with a message in his hand.

"It's for you, m'lord," he announced, handing him the piece of paper.

Tom looked at it. The seal was black, and the image imprinted in the wax was a very proud looking hedgehog. He quickly opened the letter and read it.

"Is the messenger still here?" he asked.

"Yes. A young man named Jack."

"Excellent. Let him know that I'll be quite pleased to meet with the man who sent him."

"Very good, m'lord. Will you be requiring a disguise?"

"Not this time, Waltham. Just a horse. I think I'll do fine looking like myself."

The new Lord Swynmoor rode up to The Fox and Geese. A young man was standing on a ladder in front of the inn, getting the sign reattached to its pole at last. As Tom had made his way through the village, he'd seen many people hard at work, making repairs from the storm. Fence posts were being pounded back into the ground, and men seemed to be fixing roofs from one end of town to the other. There was even some work being done on the roof tiles of the church. When he passed, many villagers bowed or curtsied, calling out good wishes for his health. A red-headed young mother held her son up and pointed at the young lord as he rode by. Smiling, he waved at them in return. He was in charge of the village now, and it was important that people knew he was taking an interest in it. He tossed a coin to the boy who took the reins of his horse and walked confidently through the door of the inn. It wasn't difficult for Tom to spot Reynaud, who was wearing his bright red bard's outfit again. Patrons of The Fox and Geese had remained largely oblivious to his presence, since he'd shaved his beard and wasn't wearing his customary black clothing. He went over to the booth where his friend was sitting with a grin on his face.

"Well, if it isn't the dread Reynaud the Red," Tomlin said, plunking down across from him.

"I'm going by Roderick these days, but it is rather nice to be wearing a color again."

A barmaid came over to the table and curtsied to the new Earl of Swynmoor.

"Pleased to have your custom, m'lord," she said, giggling a little.

"Two flagons of stout with some bread and cheese, I think."

As he was reaching for the purse of money on his belt, the dark haired young man tossed two silver coins onto the table. The girl scooped them up and rushed off to get their food and drinks. Tom opened his mouth to protest, but he was quickly cut off by Reynaud.

"I still owe you a drink," he said, "From when we met at The Wounded Soldier."

At that, he simply nodded, accepting the other man's generosity.

"So, are you enjoying lording it over the neighborhood these days?"

"It's a bit odd," he replied, "And sudden. It has its good points, I suppose."

"How was the funeral?"

"Aunt Jilona organized it, so it was all rather excessive. I think I still may have a touch of heartburn from the leftovers. I don't know how you people eat so much shellfish, where you come from. I'm not sure my digestion will ever entirely recover."

The other young lord chuckled as the girl came back with a pair of nearly overflowing pewter mugs and a plate of the requested food. Offering another brief curtsey to Tomlin, she giggled behind her hand again before retreating behind the bar to stare at him from a distance.

"It's things like that I don't think I'll ever get used to. People at the funeral I've known since I was a little boy were bowing and scraping to me."

"I have enough brothers that I don't think I'll ever have the privilege."

"If you can call it that," he said, ruefully.

Reynaud raised his flagon, tilting it slightly toward the other man.

"To the new Earl of Swynmoor. May his life be long, his cup be full, and his bed seldom empty."

Each of them took a long drink, banging their mugs down on the table with satisfaction when they'd finished.

"That ale is fantastic," said the dark haired lord, "You were right about this place. The last time we were here, I was too busy dancing with Topaz to even finish a drink."

"How is she these days? I take it that you're married now."

"I'm the luckiest man in Highreach. Both of our families are furious, of course."

"Why would they be? She comes from a perfectly respectable clan, and they're pretty well off. And I'd have thought the Stonemonts would be overjoyed for her to make it down the aisle with anyone. No offense, of course."

"None taken. Well, to begin with, our relatives are far from pleased that they weren't consulted beforehand. My father is outraged at me, as usual -- this time because he'd had some woman already picked out, though he didn't bother to tell me about it, of course."

Tom laughed, "Ugh -- the dreaded arranged marriage! I'm sure you're well out of it. She was probably twice your age and had two heads."

"As far as the Stonemonts are concerned, my family's stock has fallen to an unacceptable level. Since we suffered a crushing defeat at the hands of the Swynmoors, we're in disgrace. Her relatives are positively mortified about being associated with us, but they can't do anything about it."

"How dreadful! Where will the two of you live, if everyone's so steamed?"

"Oh, here and there -- at least until someone gets over his fit of pique long enough to let us have some family money again. Topaz seems to think that once there's a new little Evensea running around on tiny feet, they'll relent."

"As tall as that girl is, your children might have enormous feet."

"You mustn't say things like that, Moondown," he paused, thinking, "Hrm, I suppose I'll have to start calling you Swynmoor again. She's my wife, so I'll have to challenge you to a duel if you insult her."

"Sorry -- I had quite a lot of resentment toward Lady Topaz, while my aunt was trying to shove me into a wedding costume next to her. It wasn't the poor girl's fault, but it's rather hard to stop feeling like that, even though that she's safely hitched to you now."

"Much to the chagrin of many."

"What are you going to do about money until your relatives come around?"

"We'll travel through Highreach for a while, taking in the sights. I thought I'd try my luck as a sell-sword for a year or two. If that skill's not wanted, my wife could do a marvelous job as a dancing instructor for young ladies."

"Good heavens -- how does she feel about all of this?"

"Topaz doesn't seem to mind. She never got on with her family, you know. They were always giving her a hard time about her height and making her wear ridiculous clothes she hated. It's a bit of a relief for her to be free of them, for now."

"Well, I wish the two of you every good fortune."

He raised his glass for another toast, and Reynaud cheerfully touched it with his own. The young men laughed together for a while longer, drinking ale and eating bread and cheese. It was with more than a touch of regret that the dark haired lord took his leave. He genuinely liked Swynmoor and considered him a friend, despite the unfortunate circumstances under which they'd met. He walked through the village, thinking of opportunities he'd lost and other chances he'd recently taken. Soon, he found himself at the church once again. He opened the doors, waving at Hubert as he knelt at his daily work, maintaining the candles. The brown-robed man nodded as Reynaud made his way down into the basement. A very tall girl dressed in grey from head to foot was waiting for him.

"There you are," she said, smiling, "I was starting to get worried."

"I would never leave you for very long, dearest," he replied.

He kissed his wife fully on the lips, thoroughly reassured that he was exactly where he should be.

Garrok and Izir were headed in the same direction, so they decided to travel together. The two generals had been through enough together that they'd been able to set their differences aside. Mounted on their fearsome bicorns, they rode next to each other, making their leisurely way south. Reynaud the Black had paid them well for their services, and plenty of gold coins were jingling in their saddlebags. Their families would be even more pleased to see them than usual. On the third day of their journey, the warmth of the day made Garrok sleepy. He let the reins of his bicorn become slack as his eyelids grew heavy. Soon, his head was hanging down, and he was snoring in the saddle. Undirected, his mount bumped up against the Fomorian's and pushed it to the side of the road.

"Eeeeyah!" Izir shouted, "You insult me!"

Too late, the ogre's eyes jerked open, and he took hold of the reins again.

"It was an accident. Bicorn did it on his own. Sorry."

The Fomorian shook his large, grey head.

"No, it not accident! You tell him push me!"

The two former mercenaries halted their mounts in the middle of the road, glaring at each other dangerously.

"I am not a liar. I said sorry. We are friends now -- you should trust me!"

Izir dismounted heavily, the impact of his feet stirring up dust.

"We not real friends. You say travel together so you take gold when I sleep!"

The ogre also got down from his bicorn, nostrils flaring.

"I am not a liar! I am not a thief! Ogres have honor!"

"Honor this!" the Fomorian shouted.

He leaned forward, so that their faces were inches apart, then he belched horribly, his breath like sulfur. Garrok shouted and pushed hard on the other general's breastplate with both palms, his metal studded gloves ringing against the Fomorian's armor. Izir was bigger than the ogre, but the dirt road was rutted and unstable. He fell on his back, and the other former mercenary went down on top of him, his fist connecting with the grey, warty jaw. They rolled around in the dust, punching, kicking, and even biting. The bicorns watched for a while, then wandered over to the side of the road together to crop some grass. Silently, they continued to observe the fight, rolling their unsettling red eyes, which had struck fear into the hearts of many. Silly two-legged creatures, they communicated wordlessly with each other.

EPILOGUE

Despite the dim light, Kerris made her way effortlessly down the uneven steps of the abbey's basement. She had, after all, spent nearly every moment of her life in this building, so she knew even the most obscure corners of the place. More than ever, she now understood that the abbey would always be her home. This time, she bypassed the pickle barrels that remained after the rest had been sold or used to pay taxes. Having proven that she could make pickled peppers successfully, the sisters had encouraged her to help with the wine. She went over to the considerably larger barrels that were used for the fermentation of grape juice, humming contentedly. It was a Saturday, and Tom would be there soon. He had written and visited her faithfully each week, and they'd continued to get to know each other better.

The wine barrels were all lying on their sides, resting comfortably next to each other. Kerris fished the clean vial out of her apron pocket and pulled the stopper from the side of a barrel that faced the ceiling. Her hand fit through the opening with ease, and she took a sample of the honeyed white wine. Firmly replacing the cork, she went over to the low stool that had been left next to the high-set window. She stepped up on it, then raised the wine filled vessel higher than her head, so she could make use of what little light was able to penetrate through the rippled window glass. The Foundling girl peered at the pale yellow liquid, swirling it around, trying to determine whether it had gotten thick or cloudy. She'd narrowed her eyes and was squinting at it, when she heard Sister Goldrose's unmistakably heavy footsteps coming down the stairs. The nun's robes swished as she walked through the basement, coming toward the Foundling girl. Soon she was standing next to her, looking up at the vial, as well.

"How's the wine coming along?" she asked.

"I think it's all right. It seems to be clear enough, anyhow."

Without any warning, the nun reached up and grabbed the vial from Kerris' hand. After smelling its contents, she tipped the liquid into her mouth and held it there for a few moments, sampling its taste on her tongue before swallowing. She stood still, eyes closed reflectively.

"I suppose it will do well enough," she said, at last, "Not bad for your first batch, though it could do with a bit less honey."

"Yes, Sister."

"That's not really why I brought my old bones down here, though. There's something I have to say to you before your young man arrives."

"He's not really --"

"Hush, girl. If that boy isn't yours, I don't know who he belongs to. He stares at you like a lost dog."

Kerris sighed. There was no point in trying to talk Sister Goldrose out of an idea, once it had gotten into her head.

"What do you need to talk to me about?" she asked, changing the subject.

"It's something that will take more than a moment or two. You'd best come upstairs to my room, where it's more comfortable. And private, as well."

Getting down from the stool, she nodded. She couldn't imagine what the nun had to say to her that was confidential, so she was naturally curious. The Foundling girl followed her out of the basement and up several flights of steps, noting that she was taking as many of the back ways as possible. Strangely, it had never occurred to her when she'd been trying to sneak around that the sisters knew all of the seldom used stairways and corridors, as well. It made sense, though -- many of them had been here for decades before she'd even been born. The older woman eventually led her into a small, austere room that contained a single bed with a small wooden triangle hanging above it, a clothes chest, a desk, and two rather hard chairs. She took one of them and gestured for the girl to sit in the other.

"I had a letter from Brother Eustace yesterday," she began.

Kerris stiffened with apprehension, as if a glass of cold water was about to be thrown in her face.

"What did he say?" she asked carefully.

"He told me about a barrel of pickles that he had to throw into the river."

"Oh no!" the Foundling girl wailed, "He said that he wouldn't tell anyone."

"Men are notoriously bad at keeping promises. Which is part of why we keep you girls locked up in here -- but I'm wandering away from the topic at hand."

"Am I in a lot of trouble? You wouldn't have me tossed out of the abbey, would you, Sister? I never meant to --"

"Of course you didn't mean any harm, but things like that have a way of hurting people in ways you'd never expect. But you already know that now."

"Yes, Sister," she said, staring at her feet.

"I didn't bring you up here to punish you or even shout at you. But plainly the time has come to tell you something important."

She looked up, an inquiring expression on her face.

"I know we've always said that we found you lying on our doorstep, wrapped in a blanket, the same way that some of the other Foundling girls came to us," she paused, taking a breath before continuing, "That's not really true."

"It isn't?"

"No, dear. I know who your mother is and your father, as well. She came to the abbey when you were about to be born, and I caught you with my own hands."

Kerris tried to form words in response, but nothing emerged from her mouth but a squeak that sounded like it could have come from a startled mouse.

"I'm sure you want to know why your parents couldn't keep you," Sister Goldrose continued.

She nodded, still unable to speak.

"You're too young to remember it, but times were very different then. A terrible priest had gained a great deal of power, and he became one of the chief bishops. He preached that magic was evil and anyone who practiced it should be killed. Nearly all the wizards in Highreach sailed east, where no one would harm them, though there were a few very brave souls who went into hiding."

"And my parents were --"

"Wizards. Both of them. They were about to go East, as well, when your mother realized she was pregnant. She wouldn't risk the life of her baby by going on a dangerous sea voyage, so they waited until you were born to leave. But they wanted you to stay in Highreach. They had this foolish idea that if you were raised as a normal girl, you might become one."

"So they left me here."

"I told them it was no use. A baby that has two parents with magic powers grows up to be a wizard, just as a colt becomes a horse. But they gave you to us, all the same. I'd always meant to tell you when you got older, but there never seemed to be a good time. Now that the incident with the pickles has happened, though, I couldn't let things go on like this. You had to know, before you accidentally did something terrible."

"Do you know my real last name? It's not really Seaborn, is it?"

"No, that's just what we called you to throw off the wizard-killers. It's

Aurea -- a surname that magic folk have proudly called their own for generations. The name Kerris came from your mother's lips, though. Apparently, it's what your grandmother was called."

"Where did my parents go? Have you ever had a letter from them?"

The older woman shook her head.

"We never heard from them again, though if you ever decide to look for your mother and father, knowing your real name will probably help. All the sisters here love you like our own daughter, Kerris, and we'd hate to see you go. But whether you decide to become a nun, marry that young lord, or sail East after your parents, we'll always be on your side."

The Foundling girl rose from the hard chair and kissed Sister Goldrose on the cheek, unshed tears stinging her eyes.

"Thank you," she said, "Thank you for telling me. I'm not sure what I'll do, but at least I'll be able to think it through knowing everything I should."

She left the nun's room, nearly running down the stairs and out of the abbey. Reaching the back gate, she squeezed between a pair of metal bars that had been bent long ago by some unknown force. Kerris couldn't imagine how many girls over the years had slipped out to do exactly what she was about to do now. After running for a few minutes, she came to the edge of a rocky cliff that provided a magnificent view of the sea. It pounded against the rocks, far below, making a crashing sound. She stood near the edge, gazing at the grey-green water. For the first time, she knew her parents were out there, somewhere across this ocean. Perhaps, someday soon, she'd set off to find them.

One thing was now certain. She wasn't just a Foundling girl with nothing but peasant blood running through her veins. Generations ago, wizards had walked proudly beside the nobles of Highreach as equals. If she married the Earl of Swynmoor, she wouldn't be coming to him as nothing more than a poor girl that he'd generously chosen to elevate, in order to join his aristocratic family. Nodding in satisfaction, she took one more look at the sea before she turned away. Tom would be arriving soon. When he came, she would be ready.

ABOUT THE AUTHOR

Joelle received a B.A. in creative writing from Carnegie Mellon University and a master's degree in library science from San Jose State University. Her first book, *The Virgin Mary in the Perceptions of Women*, was published by McFarland & Company in 2008. When she writes fiction, she prefers to focus on fantasy/sf, as she has been a huge fan of those genres since before J.K. Rowling made them socially acceptable. Her work has also appeared in several internationally distributed magazines, including *Renaissance*, *Pirates*, and most regularly, *Faerie*. Over time, she has come to understand that books, cats and tea are all she really needs to be happy.

www.ingramcontent.com/pod-product-compliance
Lightning Source LLC
Chambersburg PA
CBHW030546130626
46552CB00006B/2442